ESCAPE

THE SEA

COPYRIGHT

© Copyright 2017 by G. Bailey.
All rights reserved.
This is a work of fiction. Names, characters, places, brands, media, and incidents are either the product of the author's imagination or are used fictitiously. The author acknowledges the trademark owners of various products, bands, and/or stores referenced in this work of fiction, which have been used without permission. The publication/use of these trademarks is not authorized, associated with, or sponsored by the trademark owners.

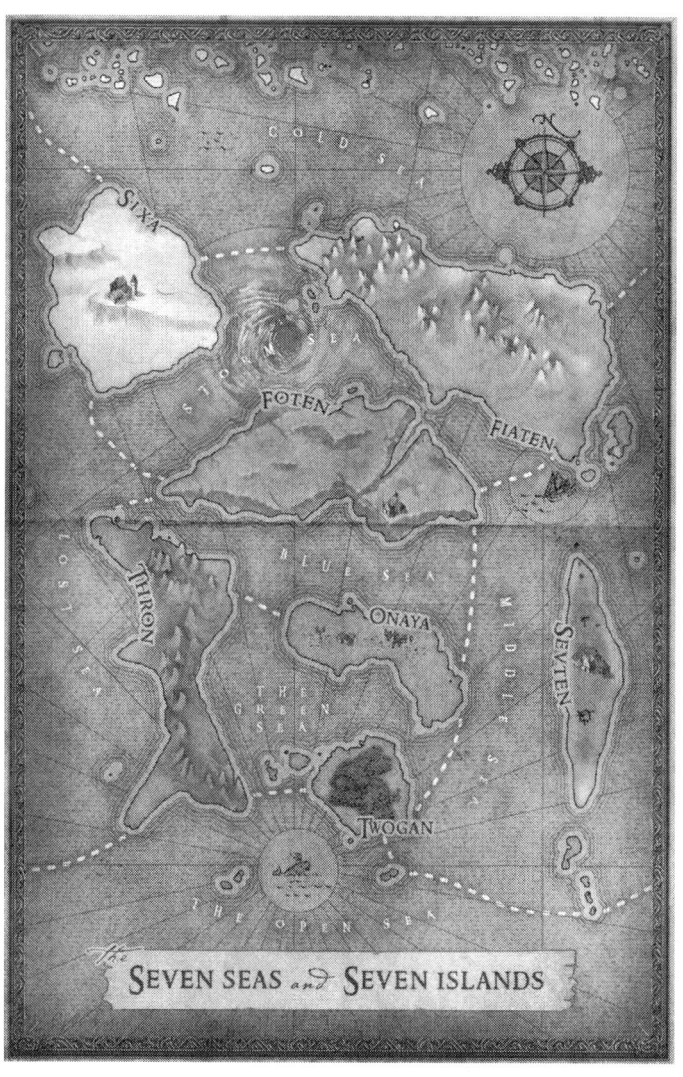

DESCRIPTION

Seven towns. Seven seas. The seven council. The seven words every person lives by.

The sea is lost, pirates are death.

Cassandra should have been killed at birth, like all the other children who have powers like her. The changed ones.
The ones who started the war, lost the seas, and killed millions with their gifts.
Lucky for Cassandra, her father is on the council. One of the seven rulers of her large town and has kept her hidden her entire life.
When she is seen for the first time, she has no choice but to run, and the only place she can go is to the sea.

To the pirates and a certain death.
At least, that is what she thinks. When she meets six handsome pirates and they take her on board their ship, she learns about a whole new world.
If only she can protect her heart when they all desire to own it.
This is a reverse harem trilogy.

For all the people that dream of pirates, mermaids, dragons, and magic.
This is for you, because I dream about them too.

PROLOGUE

I stand on the edge of the cliff, holding the blood-covered crown. The crown we fought so long to get. The crown that will win the war. I glance around at the men I love, each one of them I would die for. My pirates are fighting around me on the battlefield, keeping me alive as I face the king alone. This was always the plan, the only one that would work. The ground shakes as more screams fill the night. I can't look away from the king to see if anyone I know is dying. If anyone I love is.

Everything we have fought for has led us to this moment, and I won't let them down.

We don't say any words to each other, words are not needed. He knew this was coming, and the war around us is proof. The king started this, not me. I was chosen to stop this.

"You will never save the seas," the king sneers at me after a long silence between us.

"I don't need to. The Sea God will save us all," I say, my voice loud as the wind howls, and lightning fills the skies.

"What did you promise him in return?" he shouts back at me. I look the king over, remembering every cruel thing he has done to me, the people he has taken from me, and the deaths he has caused.

"Your death," I say and lift the crown, placing it on my head.

I

CASSANDRA

"Name the seven islands of Calais," Miss Drone orders me, like I haven't been taught them my whole life. Every week, she asks me these questions. I will never see any other island than the one I am stuck on, so I don't see the point in knowing all their names.

"Onaya, Twogan, Thron, Foten, Fiaten, Sixa, and Sevten," I answer. *It's like someone has counted to seven, and named an island after each number.*

"Who rules all the islands?" she asks as she reads the paper I wrote for her this week. It's filled with my opinions on the last book she gave me to read, a book about the seven seas.

"King Dragon and his queen, Riah," I answer. I almost want to add that the pirates own the waters, but I know she won't like me saying that. It's not worth the argument that would follow. The king ignores the pirates, and the pirates are said to ignore him. The king chose the seven families to rule each island after he took his throne, then he left us alone on the islands. We only see the king once a year when he visits all the islands with his queen. Well, I've never seen him, his queen, or his children. Only the seven council members get to see them.

There's only one law the king regularly reminds everyone to follow: kill the changed ones, or he sends his guards to the island and kills them anyway.

"Tell me the final words you need to know," she asks in her cold tone.

"Never go near the sea, never leave the walls. The sea is lost, pirates are death," I repeat back to my teacher. Miss Drone believes telling me the same thing every time I see her will make sure I understand her. She really has no idea. She nods like she thinks she's done her job today. Those are always the words she says last to me, every week at the same time, the same hour. The same senseless rules.

ESCAPE THE SEA

My whole life is full of rules that mean nothing to me.

"Cassandra, are you listening to me?" Miss Drone asks in a sharp tone. I glance up from my seat, looking at her. I don't know her first name. She never told me, and I never asked anyone to tell me. My father always calls her Miss Drone, and her daughter calls her Mother. Miss Drone has light-blonde hair that's cut short, and she's wearing an old dress, covered in holes. She is a widow from the poor side of the island. My father says she's lucky, lucky not to be dead or on the streets, and that's why she doesn't tell anyone about me. That's why she has taught me my whole life for the tiny amount of food my father gives her. I guess it's because food is treasured here on Onaya, where we have little. People can't leave, because the seas are full of pirates, and even if you did get to the other islands, they are in no better condition. No one can trade between the islands. The only way we know people are even alive on them is by talking to the couple of people who make it to our shore. They come looking for a home and food, but are sadly disappointed. We grow very little on our farms; the land is dying, and people don't know why. It's said to be like this on every island, and it gets worse every single year.

"Yes, of course I am," I say. I fake a smile at her, and she relaxes in her seat. Miss Drone is terrified of me. Everyone that has ever been near me is. My father has only let me meet three people in my life. Him, Miss Drone, and her daughter, Everly. Everly keeps me from going insane with boredom, and Miss Drone teaches me things I apparently need to know. Like how the seas are lost, and everyone dies out there.

I don't know why I need to know anything when I can never leave my house, or the grounds surrounding it.

"Well then, I will be off. Everly will be over after school," she says as she stands and walks towards the door. I wait until she shuts it before I walk towards the window.

I can see my whole town from this window. It's striking. The island is shaped like a foot, or that's how I like to think of it. The brown state house stretches like a line straight down the middle, towards my large house and the large acre that surrounds it. Our house is the biggest on the island because of who my father is—one of seven council members. They always get the best of everything.

There are three others houses on my row, but they are far smaller. I have been told there are three more on the other side of the island, too, the same size as the smaller ones next to ours. I don't know why my father has the biggest house on the island, but he does. I only know what my father has told me. I know that they house the other council members and their families. The council makes all the decisions on the island, everything from enforcing the laws, to how much food they think people need to eat.

The people worship them and do anything they ask, because they give them food. They keep them safe and make sure that no pirates get into their town.

If only they knew about me, his secret, they wouldn't love him like they do. My reflection shines back at me from the window. My brown hair is in waves around my face, with little feathers braided in and tiny plaits I've added when I've gotten bored. My hazel eyes match my hair, in my opinion making me look normal. The only thing that isn't normal is the upside-down, black triangle on my forehead.

My mark; the very thing that makes me hide. The very thing I wish I could get rid of, so I could have a normal life. A life where I could walk out of the house.

"Cassandra, come here," my father shouts up the stairs.

After one more glance at my reflection, I leave my room.

2

CASSANDRA

"I have to go away for three nights, Cassandra. I'm travelling to the other side of Onaya," my father says the second I walk into his office. The old decor matches the grumpy old man look my father gives me. My father's once-brown hair is grey, and his beard is slowly matching. The room is stuffy and needs cleaning, like a lot of the house. I try to clean it, but he goes mad. The place is a shrine to my mother, and he doesn't like anything changed in it. Everything is the same as when she died in childbirth, died giving my father me, his only child and one he has to hide. I know that my father cares for me, but he doesn't know what to do with me anymore. He looks down at the piles of old, yellow rolls of parchment, his hands folded into tight fists. He doesn't want to go and leave me here, I know that. My father is around fifty with a receding hair line and round stomach from all the food he eats, and his white shirt stretches to keep him in it. The only thing I think I inherited from him was my light-brown hair. My mother's was black and her skin was darker than mine, or so I've been told. I'm very pale compared to my father's tanned skin, but I believe it's more from the lack of sunlight than what I was born with. I only get to go outside at night or late evening when no one is around.

"I will stay inside, and I'll be fine," I say as I wave a hand at him and sit on the window seat instead of one of the spare chairs in the room. I have to sit close to the windows, because otherwise I feel trapped in here, or at least that's what I tell myself. My father doesn't question my choice of seats like he used to. He hasn't since I told him about feeling trapped in this house.

"I have never left you this long before, but now that you are eighteen, I believe you can be alone for a short amount of time," he says and picks up a bowl of soup. I watch him eat it, wondering how many people in this town would kill for one hot meal like that when this is likely his fourth one today. My father could choose to eat less and give it to the worst off, but he wouldn't. He thinks I eat as much as he does. I don't. I hide my food and give it to Everly. She takes it to the people who need it on the poor side of town. Everly tells me how bad it is, how the people die from starvation or they go to the water. I'm not sure which is worse, but I only eat one meal a day because of it.

"I'm old enough to be alone for three days. You are rarely home these days, you're always working. There isn't much of a difference," I tell him, my tone harsher than I usually speak to him.

He picks up on it. "A new attitude seems to have developed as well," he tells me.

I look away and out the window, "I'm sorry–"

He cuts me off with his harsh words spoken with anger, "You should be. I saved you from being killed as a baby, hid you your entire life, and fed you, because I loved your mother. If she was here–" he snaps at me, throwing his bowl across the room. It smashes into the wall right next to me. I watch the red soup drip down the wall as the room goes silent.

I just turn and plaster on a fake smile, one I have become perfect at showing. My father has a temper, and it's best to just be nice to him and let him calm down. "Father, I didn't mean to—" I get out before he interrupts.

"I killed another man today, a gardener who saw you and was stupid enough to tell his family," he tells me, and sickness fills my throat. I don't say anything for a while, I just stare at him. I don't want to know how he killed him, although he likely used a sword. We are one of the few families who have any swords, as it's a sign of being well off. Also, no one would ever tell the council about an unusual killing. Everly says they always know it was one of them. They all have weapons like my father does.

"The family?" I ask, my voice betraying my emotions when it cracks.

"Also dead. No one can know about you, so don't look at me like that," my father snaps. I don't respond as I look at the dated red rug on the floor. It has yellow designs drawn into it, and I trace the yellow circles with my eyes for a long time, the silence in the room deafening.

"The things I have done to keep you alive would haunt you, Cassandra. I only ask that you watch your tongue around me," he says, and I nod, words leaving me. Everly told me of the people that go missing, I have everyone written down in a book upstairs. The ones I know about, anyway.

The guilt does haunt me. They died, because they knew I was alive.

"The king and his family are coming in two weeks. I need for you to behave while I work," he says, and I nod. I knew they would be coming soon. I keep track of their visits on my calendar upstairs.

"Cassandra, leave me. I wish to be alone," my father tells me, and I look up at his dark blue eyes, seeing the emptiness of them. *How many men and women can you kill before it destroys you?*

I stand and walk out of the office, not looking back at my father. I know he means well, but we are so different. How he sees people and life is different than how I do. Maybe it's because I'm locked up in here, or maybe it's because I spend all my time watching people from windows. Maybe he is just how men are, being that he is the only one I've ever spoken to.

The only one I will ever get to speak to if my life doesn't change, and I know it never can, it never will.

3

CASSANDRA

"Cassy, where are you?" Everly's voice shouts throughout the house. I move away from my place near the window in the kitchen as she bangs the door open. I smile when I see her head of blonde swirls as she slams into the room. Everly is the very meaning of happiness. She has a row of freckles on her nose and cheeks, bright sea-blue eyes, and is a little shorter than I am.

"That door is always getting stuck," she huffs and straightens up. Everly is just as thin as me, but it isn't by choice for her, and I hate that. No matter what life throws at her, she is always happy. I don't know why I can't be more like her. She walks straight over to me and throws her arms around me.

"You look sad. Why?" she asks as she leans back, her hands on my shoulders.

"Another argument with my father. He's going away tonight," I say, not wanting to tell her that he killed a family. I'm sure she will hear about it soon enough. Everly believes my father is a monster, and she isn't wrong, not in my eyes. The names of the people he has killed to keep my secret run through my mind. I know he never offers them a deal to save themselves. I'm sure some of them would have sworn not to say anything about me to save themselves and their families. Or gotten on a boat and left the island. My father could have made them leave.

"Ah, don't take it to heart," she waves a hand at me. Everly has on a dirty-white, long tunic, tied in the middle with a belt. She works in the fields just outside of town, where most of the food is grown. Everly tells me stories of the handsome men she works with, and they are all I ever seem to hear from her recently. I understand it. Well, the *idea* of love and attraction. I just have never had the chance to feel that way about a man. Turning eighteen yesterday didn't change those thoughts.

"I know, Ev," I say, and she grins. I pick up an apple from the side that I was going to eat and hand it to her. She doesn't say anything but takes it with a nod. She can't refuse food when she doesn't know where the next meal comes from, and she has to work all day. Apples are rare, even for my father, but we have our own tree in the gardens.

"Was my mother alright with you today?" Everly asks me around a bite of the apple.

"Same stuff, another day," I say and go back to my window. The view of the town is slightly different from here. It's sundown now, the two moons slowly appearing in the sky. The sky is lit up different shades of orange, with little bits of pink wiped across it. I want to say it's my favourite part of the day, but it's not. I prefer the night, when the bright stars come out.

"I have an idea," Everly suddenly says, and I glance back her. Everly's ideas are rarely safe and always involve sneaking me out of here. She doesn't believe I have to hide, and she doesn't realise how many people have been killed because they saw me. When we were seven, she came up with the idea to climb the nearest wall and see the sea at night. We did and a couple saw us. They told people around the town the next day about seeing two strange girls. My father killed them for that, even if they didn't see, or know about, my mark. I found out because Miss Drone shouted at my father, and I heard the whole thing. They were close friends of Miss Drone's. It didn't matter in the end, because my father simply offered to kill her and Everly if she wanted to say anything. I'm glad Miss Drone walked away.

"I am not leaving the house and putting that stuff on," I say, pulling my thoughts back to Everly and her foolish ideas. My father brought me some thick paste that covers my mark and blends in with my skin. I use it sometimes when I leave the house at night to go into the gardens. There isn't a lot of it, so I have to be careful in case there's a time when I will actually need it.

"You are, because we are going to a party," Everly says with a massive smile on her face.

"A party? Have you gone mad?" I ask her, and she shakes her head, her curls flying everywhere. Everly's hair is out of control most the time–like her personality.

"No, I have not. We will go tomorrow night," she says and takes a last bite of the apple.

"What if it rains? That stuff isn't waterproof," I tell her, and she chuckles.

"It doesn't rain anymore. You know that," she says, and I know she's right. I'm being silly to think it might rain. There hasn't been any rain for four months now, and there isn't a dark cloud to be seen in the sky. The farmers are now using sea water to feed the plants, and it's killing them slowly. The lack of rain has also caused our water supplies to get low. My father says we need a few storms soon or something drastic will have to be done. I dread to know what that might be.

"It might," I shrug a shoulder, not meeting her eyes.

"If so, the whole village would be staring at the sky, not you, Cass. Plus, we will go at night, so no one will see you," she says with a grin. I mentally sigh and look over at her. I know she won't give up, and it's only one night.

"I don't know–" I get out, and she cuts me off with a wave of her hand.

"You will, and you can meet some people. Maybe some men," she winks, and I laugh. If only meeting a man would be the worst thing that could happen to me, but I know it is not in my future. Any man would take one look at my mark and run the other way, as fast as they could if they were smart. I'm guessing if I had children, they would be changed like me, but it's only a guess. I would never risk having children or falling in love. The result would only be death, as death chases me for my mark.

"No, I don't think so, Ev. I'll live with your stories of handsome strangers and what I read in my books," I say, and she laughs loudly.

"Reading is not the same as living, Cass, and you need to live," she says and throws the apple core into a bin as I think over her words. Who knows how long it could be until my father goes away again?

It's only one night and one party. I can talk to some people and have enough memories to keep me going for a while. It's difficult to be locked in this house all the time, talking to only three people, and having only the stars for company at night. I'm eighteen and tired of living a life being hidden. One night would help that, just one night.

A night to give me something to dream about other than the stars.

4

CASSANDRA

"All done," Everly pulls her hand back with the sponge and hands me a little mirror. My hair is half up, with two feathers at the ends of two little plaits on each side of my head. My mark is covered up, and instead, Everly has drawn a red line on my lips like hers. It's apparently the fashion, and everyone does it. I wouldn't know, but I trust her.

"Thank you, Ev," I say, and she nods at me with a cheeky grin. She looks lovely in her lacy dress; it's a little like mine and fits her well. Her dress is black, whereas mine is a light-blue. My father bought it for me. He said my mother had one like it, and he just wanted to get me a gift. The blue dress is full of stitched holes, and it dips a little low on my chest. I put a silver necklace on that had belonged to my mother. It has three upside-down triangles along the chain, and it's funny how the shapes look similar to my mark. I run my fingers across the necklace, and I wonder how my mother would have treated me if she were still here. Would she have encouraged me leaving the house? Or would she have kept me hidden?

"Let's go," Everly says as she takes my hand and we walk through the empty house. Every single one of the rooms we walk through is crowded with things that have been here for years. We pass through the front room, and I can't help but look around. I look at the two loungers and the big, old paintings on the wall. The painting is of farmers in the fields, an everyday scene, but it's beautifully painted. My father doesn't know who painted it; he said it's just always been in the house since he was a child. I glance across the room, knowing that it is the cleanest one out of all the rooms in the house. The dust is still thick in here, and there are still piles of books on the floor, but at least you can see the floor. The house is hard to stay in and every day I think, *if only my father would let me clean it out and throw some things away*. Everly pulls the door to the entrance hall open, and we walk out of the dusty room.

Everly swings the front door open. It bangs against the wall, and she laughs with me. She is far too excited for this night. I take a deep breath when we get outside, enjoying the clean air. The outside smells like grass, and the warm air flitters around my dress. I look up at the familiar stars, how they shine a certain light over the dark night and surround the large moon. Leaving the house means I see all the stars from a different angle. She pulls my arm, which is hooked in hers, snapping my attention back to her. We walk down to the side of the house and towards the stables to get our horses.

"Come on," Everly shouts as she gets on her horse. I go to the other horse tied up next to her. She is my father's horse, but he isn't using her tonight. I named her Sea, for her bright, sea-coloured eyes, and because she didn't have a name from my father. Sea huffs at me as I stroke her head and grab the reins. After I pull myself on top of her, Everly rides off with a laugh. I follow, and we ride away from my father's house. I'm glad I learned how to ride a horse by riding up and down the stables at night for years. I force myself not to look back at the large house. I know if I look back, the guilt of what I'm doing will get to me. This is a big risk, and my father could suffer if people found out about me. They would kill me or hand me over to the king. I'm not sure which one would be worse, but I have always imagined it's being given to the king. My father speaks little of his visits with him, but Everly tells me things. Like how the council members take their daughters or wives to the king, and how many do not return. She says the people know the king kills them for sport, but there isn't anything that can be done about it. In a way, my mark may have saved me from my father taking me to see the king.

I slow Sea down when we get to the metal gates, which are wide open. The gates are usually locked, and I don't even want to ask how Everly managed to get them open. I'm just going to assume she stole her mother's key and is going to put it back before she notices. We leave the gates open as we leave. No one usually comes up here, so it should be safe. No one is mad enough to break into one of the council houses. The council members are not known for being kind. They are known for killing entire families for just stealing extra food.

My father says it's because they have such little food that they must keep the population low. It's disgusting, and if he really felt bad about it at all, he wouldn't eat the large amount of food that he does.

We ride down the uneven, stone road. The horse's shoes clicking against the stone is the only sound that can be heard, other than the quiet wind in the trees. When we hit the start of town and the row of houses, Everly slows down, and I copy her speed. The houses are small, with brown bricks and thatched roofs. Some have wooden doors, but many just have fabric hanging over the hole where the door should be. There are people huddled by the doors in the street, thick blankets thrown over them, and their empty eyes meet mine. I have to look away, as I can't help them. *I wish I could.* I click my horse's reins to move forward and stop next to Everly. She smiles at me and then looks forward as we cross a few people. I hold my breath, wondering if they will say something about my mark before I remember it's covered up with the face paste.

The people don't even glance our way, and I let go of the breath I was holding. Everly says more and more travellers are turning up these days, so no one bats an eye at a stranger moving down the streets. It's just hard to believe until you see it. I've spent so much of my life hidden, I don't know how to just act normal. I'm surprised to see that most people have horses as we ride past them. I know they are the only way to travel the island, and that we breed them, but my father says they are dying. The horses don't have enough fresh food anymore, because the grass is dying from the lack of rain.

Everly turns down a smaller road, which leads further out of the main row of houses. The house we stop at is near the walls that have the Green Sea on the other side. You can even hear the sea in the wind, as it whistles and blows. The Green Sea is dead, full of poison. It has an awful, thick fog over it, making it impossible to see much through it. I've only seen it once, when I snuck out of the house with Everly. The Middle Sea is on the other side of the island, and Everly said the water is a deep-blue. She says it's cold, but people still swim in it sometimes.

I get off my horse and walk her over to the line of other horses that are tied up. Everly ties her brown horse next to mine while I wait. There's water in front of them, so they'll be happy for a little while. I take Everly's arm as we walk up to the small wooden house. The house has seen better days, and the thatched roof is nearly falling off. The front door is wide open, and the sound of someone playing music is in the background. I try not to stare at the couple in the small room we come in to. It's only them in here, and they are all over each other. Their mouths are glued together, and they're pulling each other's clothes off. They're both wearing work clothes like Everly wears. That kind of passion is something I've never seen before, only heard of, and it shocks me enough that I quickly look away as Everly pulls me through another door. The door leads outside again, and I can see the person playing the music sitting on some planks of wood. The man is playing some kind of flute, the sound is nice, and the tune is louder than I would expect from such a small instrument. There are twenty or more people standing around or dancing while they smile. It makes me smile, because it's so normal. *I'm at a normal party, with normal people.*

"Come on, live a little, Cass," Everly whispers in my ear, and I grin at her. We make our way over, and Everly grabs both my hands. She swings with me in circles, and I laugh. A few people join in our dance, and she stops to link my arm with hers and spin us around in circles. We stop after a while, and I walk over to a gate, while I watch the people as Everly talks to them. A few people glance at me, but my breath catches when I meet the gaze of a pair of sea-blue eyes.

The eyes belong to a handsome man's face. My eyes travel over him, seeing his strong jawline is covered with a small, brown beard that matches his messy brown hair. The man is tall, taller than most of the men here, and his skin is tanned like he's in the sun a lot. I don't move as he walks over to me, looking me over closely until he stops right in front of me. He tilts his head to the side.

"Where do they hide pretty girls like you?" he asks with a big smile spreading across his lips. He has on slightly different clothes than most of the people here, as he is wearing brown trousers and a dark black coat.

"Your first sentence to me was a compliment and a question. You're good at this, aren't you?" I ask him, my voice sarcastic, and he laughs.

"Good at what, *pretty girl*?" he asks, taking another step closer. I don't know where my braveness comes from as I flirt back with him. Maybe it's from all the romance books I've read.

"You don't need me to answer that, *pretty boy*," I say and earn a deep laugh from him. The man moves the final step closer, our bodies inches apart, and I turn my head up to meet his blue eyes that look so much brighter up close. We both are still as we stare at each other. I'm so close to him that I can tell that he smells like water. *How strange.*

"Dante, we have to go," a man shouts from the house, and Dante steps away from me. I take a deep breath as I watch him walk away, back towards the house. He glances back as he opens the back door, our eyes meet again, and he smiles before he walks out.

I watch the party for a while, but no one else tries to talk to me. I spot Everly chatting to a man about her age. His hand is on her arm, and she's smiling widely up at him. This must be the man she's been telling me about, the one she likes. Everly told me she met a man at work, a man who makes her smile and laugh. He is very handsome, so I can see why.

"Oh, by the seas, I'm sorry," some women says when she bumps into me as I watch Everly, and then I feel wet stuff all over my face. I wipe my eyes and glance at the slim woman with grey hair in front of me, holding a bucket of water. Her eyes widen as she looks at me, not at my eyes but my forehead. I don't need to hear her next words to know the water she just splashed all over me has made the mark appear.

"A changed one," she says in a horrified whisper

and backs away. She bumps into someone, and they both fall to the ground. I have never seen this reaction before, as no one has seen me this close up. Seen my mark. It makes all the times my father warned me not to leave the house seem more real.

"A changed one!" she screams, and lots of eyes turn to me. The fear in them is daunting, and I don't have a choice as I turn to run to the house.

"Get her!" a man shouts behind me. I don't look back as I open the door and run through the house. I run to my horse, hearing footsteps behind me, but decide I can't use the horse. She's tied up, and they will get me before I can get her loose. I run across the street instead and into a long alley where several people are wrapped up in blankets on the floor. I ignore their pleas for food as I run past, hoping I can send Everly food to give to them if I survive this. I stop when I see a door slightly open, and I slip inside, shutting the door. I turn, thankful that the house is empty, and wait until I can't hear the people following me anymore.

I slide out of the house, going back down the alley I ran up, and a hand grabs my arm pulling me into a small wall alcove. I breathe a sigh of relief when I see Everly's blonde hair, just before she pulls an old blanket over our heads. Seconds later, we hear footsteps running past us, the shouts of people screaming about finding the changed one. They will search the whole city for me, and I'll be lucky if we even make it back to my house.

"I'm sorry, Cass," Everly mumbles quietly as she takes my hand in hers. I hold back the anger I feel at the people's reaction to me. They hunt me for something they don't understand and for a power I do not have.

"It's not your fault I was born like this, Ev," I say, and she wraps an arm around me. This is no one's fault. No one who is alive, anyway. The changed one who destroyed the world in the first place is said to have died thirty years ago. We don't even know his name; only the king knows that, because it's said he was the one to kill him.

If only that man hadn't destroyed so much with his gifts, and if only people knew that we don't have these powers. Maybe the Sea God took them away when the changed one destroyed everything. If there is even a god, like my books say there is. A god of the sea, who was the first changed one. Although, it's only rumours, like everything else in my life.

The mark will always ruin my life.

5

CASSANDRA

"At least we got back." Everly laughs a little as we shut the door behind us. The trip back home was not easy, but pretending to be starving makes people look the other way. Thank the seas that Everly found that old blanket. It might have just saved my life.

"They'll search the whole island for me, Ev," I say as I pace the entrance hall by the stairs. Everly lights a candle in a lantern and puts it on the side before leaning against the wall. I can't think of how we're going to get out of this. I guess I could hide in here, but chances are, the people won't stop until they search every house. My father won't be able to keep me hidden, and he isn't here to help me. If he rode back to his house now, it would look odd.

"Your father won't let them find you," she says.

"He isn't here, Ev!" I shout, and she flinches, a reminder that even my friend is scared of me. I don't have any powers, none that can destroy the world like everyone thinks I can. I stop and stare at her as she looks away. I shouldn't have shouted at her, I know that, but I'm too nervous right now. It's not her life on the line right now. With the king so close, they will keep me alive and tortured until he arrives. There have only been two changed ones born on this island. Both were boys and were killed straight away.

"I'm sorry, Everly," I say, and she nods, still watching me with a slight bit of fear in her eyes. A banging against the front door makes us both jump and Everly motions for me to hide. I go into the under the stairs closet as Everly opens the door. The familiar sound of Miss Drone's voice drifts to me, and I sigh with relief, leaning my back against the dusty shelves. I open the door and Miss Drone is standing there, her hands on her hips, waiting for me. She looks sorry for me, an emotion I haven't seen on her face since I was a child. The last time I saw it was when I cut my foot on a bit of sharp wood in the garden. I cried and cried for my mother that day. My father simply told me to grow up and left the house. Miss Drone came a few hours later and looked after me, with that look of sympathy. I was only eight.

"We have to leave, now," she says. I look her over, noticing the big, black cloak she has on and the large, brown bag she's holding. I know she would have had this planned for a while, just in case. My father would kill me himself before handing me to the king, that much I know. So, escaping is the only other option I have.

"Where?" I ask, not really wanting to hear her answer, because I know it won't be good.

"To the sea, to Twogan," she says, confirming my worst thoughts. It's the only place I can go, to the sea.

"The Green Sea is full of poison! No one goes that way, Mother. We should send her to Foten, across the Blue Sea," Everly says in anger. The sea between Onaya and Twogan is called the Green Sea, because it is literally green and covered in fog. If you could get a boat and maybe stay afloat in the rough waters, the fog would make you lost. Foten is no better; the king lives in his castle on Foten, and it wouldn't be easy for me to hide there. The island is crawling with guards.

"They are looking for her there," Miss Drone

tells Everly, her tone affectionate, and I swallow the bitter feeling of jealously. It's a pointless emotion to feel when I know I'm leaving them both soon.

"Anyway, your father has a boat ready for you. It's been ready for years in case something happens. When he hears about you being seen, he will direct attention away from the boat," Miss Drone tells me. She places the bag on the floor and opens it up. I watch as she pulls out a blue cloak with a large hood.

"Put it on, we don't have a lot of time. The more time we waste, the more people know about you," she tells me. I take the cloak from her, looking down at the rough material and knowing when I put this on, I'll have to say goodbye to my life in this house. I glance around the room, looking at the red wallpapered walls, the piles of books on the stairs, and finally to the painting of some mountains hung on the wall. I wonder if my mother ever looked at these paintings. *I've wondered about my mother more times than I can remember.* Leaving this house feels like I'm leaving the only part of her I have ever had. I look down at the cloak one more time before I wrap it over my shoulders. Once it's tied and the hood is up, Miss Drone opens the door. Everly goes to walk out, and Miss Drone grabs her shoulder.

"No. This is my risk, not yours, Everly. You are all that I have left," she tells her, and Everly shakes her head. Her eyes flittering between me and her mother.

"You're not coming. They would kill you for knowing about me, and I can't let that happen. I wouldn't take your mother with me if there was any other way. I want to know you're safe here, because you're like a sister to me," I tell Everly, and she stares at me. She looks down at the floor, a slight sniffle escaping her before she walks over to me.

"I will see you again. The people are so wrong," Everly says, and she throws herself into my arms. "If you survive this, you will finally be free. Tonight was just a taste of the adventure you can have," she whispers in my ear, and I nod. I can't agree with her, because I know there is little chance I'll survive this.

"Thanks, Ev. I will see you again," I tell her, not wanting to upset her, and she steps away. She wipes her tears away and gives me a little smile.

"Make sure you kiss that man and live for me," I say, and she laughs.

"I love you, Cass, and I will see you again. Who knows? Maybe the changed ones won't always be hunted," she says, and I can't answer her as I turn to walk away. I step outside my house and pull the door closed, pausing with my hand on the doorknob. I want to open it and hide in my room, but I know I can't. I know there's nothing I want to take with me, nothing other than my mother's necklace which I'm already wearing. The house is full of old things, but most of them are my fathers'. There are no small paintings of my mother, no childhood mementoes I want to keep.

This house has always been more like a prison than a home for me. I let go of the doorknob and turn to face Miss Drone. She nods and turns to walk down the path to the gates.

"Do you remember what I taught you about Twogan?" she asks as we walk slowly, only the sound of distant owls can be heard in the distance.

"It's mainly covered in trees. They grow an unnatural pink, like the rest of the plants on the island. There is a small town, and they live off the fruit from the trees, but it causes their hair and eyes to change colour," I say. There has only been one person who came to Onaya from Twogan, around two years ago. Everly told me about the man's purple hair, an odd colour. The man told Everly and others about how the animals on the island are different colours, too.

"Yes, so you should be able to find shelter and feed yourself. We know you can defend yourself, if you need to," she says reminding me of all the training she did with me growing up. I can fight, I'm good with a sword, but I've only ever practised against Miss Drone and Everly. They aren't as strong as most men, and it was never a real fight. I have no doubt I wouldn't do as well against someone who was trying to hurt me. My father refused to practise fighting with me. I have practised fighting a tree in the garden, but that is of little use.

"If I make it across the sea," I say, replying to her answer as she closes the gates behind us.

"I never told you about the changed ones. The stories that are told of your kind," Miss Drone says as we take a sharp right down a deserted road. I can hear shouts in the distance, making me nervous. This road is quiet, with no houses and just trees on each side.

"The changed ones were not always feared. They were worshipped like gods. They say their powers were tied to elements, and they looked after the land," Miss Drone says, shocking me. I glance at her, but I can't see her in the darkness. I can just about see the path in front of us, thanks to the stars.

"What happened then?" I ask her because I

cannot believe that people used to like changed ones. I know nothing of my kind, other than the stories about the one who destroyed everything.

"Something went wrong when one changed one decided to misuse his power. No one is sure why he did, but there was little left after he destroyed so much," she says.

"Do you know what it was like before?" I ask her.

"The islands used to be two large lands, and the seas were travelled by many. Not just the pirates," she says as we approach the wall. The wall towers into the sky, made of thick wood, and I have no idea how she plans for us to get out. The only way I know of, is the main gate, but there is no way we would be able to get past the guards. Miss Drone pulls out a lantern from the large bag she has, and I watch as she lights the candle inside with a matchstick.

She lifts the lantern up as she walks over to a part of the wall. It has a small blue flower painted on it, but you can't see it unless you're close. She pushes against it with her shoulder, and it opens. I would have never guessed there was a door there. I follow Miss Drone through the door, and she shuts it behind her. Only a blue flower shows where the door is; the wood just fits in perfectly.

"The land was destroyed, millions of people were killed, and the few changed ones that were left, were killed by order of the new king. I don't know what you could become," Miss Drone says to me and turns to walk towards the water. A boat is tied to the edge. It looks old and not safe as the waves move it in the water. There's a small sail and two oars in the boat. She puts the lantern and the bag in as well, and then steps back.

"I believe this is just your beginning. I never spoke a word about you, never a word, because I've always known we need the changed ones back," she tells me, coming over to me and placing her hand on my shoulder.

"Why do you want us back when we destroyed the land and killed so many?" I ask, not understanding her logic.

"There is evil in every person, but there is also good. It is which part of ourselves we choose to side with that decides our future. Choose good, Cassandra, and the Sea God will reward you," she says and steps away. I watch as she walks back to the wall and disappears through the door. I turn back to the

Green Sea, the smell of salt water being carried in the breeze. The sea looks as awful as I could expect it to. The waves splash harshly against the rocks, and the fog makes it impossible to see much. I could sail straight into a rock and not see it coming. My hands shake a little as I watch the sea, knowing this is my only chance, and I force myself to remember that people have survived this trip before me.

I walk into the water, holding my dress and cloak up, but they still get wet as the waves splash, and I have to let them fall to hold on to a rock. My flat shoes are useless on the slimy rocks, and the water feels cold as it splashes against my legs. The wind howls, whipping the hood off my head, and my hair flicks around my face.

I climb into the creaky, old boat, every creak sounding louder than it should. After I undo the rope tying the boat to the shore, I undo the sail. The wind catches it and pushes us out to sea way too fast. I can't even hold on to the rope to steer it and just manage to tie it to the wooden post on the boat. I guess going straight forward is better than nothing. The fog is awful as the boat pulls us through it, and I can't see a thing as I put the oars in the holders at the sides of the boat to try and steer. *I have no idea what I'm doing.* I can't see anything other than white fog and thick, green water. I try to look up, hoping to see the stars, but even the stars are lost to me.

My heart pounds when I see a massive shadow in the fog, right in front of me. I expect it to be a large rock, and I desperately try to untie the sail, so I can steer the boat out of the way. When I look up, I can see a mermaid statue attached to the front of a large ship as it appears through the fog. It's so close, too close. The rest of the massive ship comes out of the fog as my boat seems to shoot towards it with the wind. I wrestle with the rope only to have my finger cut. It's too tight, and the wind is too strong. I know I can't move the boat in time. My small boat smashes into the side of the ship, the force knocking me out of the boat and straight into the cold water. The boat follows me under, smashing to pieces, and a part of wood catches my arm. Another bit of wood catches my necklace, ripping it off, and I reach to catch it, only to fail.

I panic as I flail my arms around, trying to get to the surface, but I can't swim with the pressure of the cloak. The cloak pulls me down by my neck as I struggle to undo the clip, but the weight is too much. The thick, green water burns my eyes as I try to open them, and I can feel the water choking me with every breath. Just as I nearly get the string undone, another thick piece of wood slams into me, and my hands drift to my sides. The sea pushes me from side to side as I watch the top of the water. The green haze and the dim stars give off a certain kind of beauty. The last thing I see is a dark shape heading straight towards me as everything goes black.

6

CASSANDRA

"Did she drink a lot of the water?" a soothing, male voice asks, and I struggle to pull my eyes open as I hear another voice talk. The room smells like herbs, and it's unfamiliar, but there is another smell that reminds me of the sea.

"No, I believe she will be fine. Have you ever seen a female changed one before?" another man replies. His voice is deep, and it sounds familiar. I try to pull myself awake to look, but I just feel sick instead.

"I will ask the others, but no, I haven't. Well, other than the queen," the man with the soothing voice replies. The room feels like it's spinning just before I hear a door shut. I wonder why the room smells like herbs. I force myself to blink my eyes open and see I'm lying down on a small bed, the sheets are white, and the pillow is soft under my head. My hair feels slightly damp as I lift my head a little. The room is all wooden, and the small, circular window gives me the biggest hint that I'm on the ship I crashed into. *It must be a pirate ship.* I move the covers a little to see that my dress and necklace are gone. Instead, I'm wearing a long, white shirt. I can't believe they changed my clothes, but I don't feel like they have hurt me. Other than the dizziness, I feel fine. I sit up quickly and look around the dimly-lit room, seeing the light is coming from the small window.

"Be careful," the soothing, deep voice of the man from before warns, and I shoot my gaze to the light-blond-haired man sitting on a desk on the other side of the room. He looks around my age, wearing a dark red shirt that shows off the middle of his chest. The shirt is tucked into black trousers, and he has a black bandana tied around his neck. He also has a necklace on, it's long and has little white shells hanging from the silver chain. His hair is medium-length, tied low at the back of his head and pulled away from his handsome face.

The man is a pirate, not handsome.

"Who are you?" I ask as we both watch each other; his face is blurring a bit, and I know it's from falling in that sea.

"Chaz, and you are?" he asks.

"Leaving," I mutter and try to stand up off the bed. I fall straight to the ground with a smack. My body feels so weak, and the room blurs again. I hear Chaz as he jumps off the desk and runs over to me. He sighs before he picks me up and lays me back on the bed. He hands me the blanket and looks me over.

"You're weak, but it should wear off soon. I gave you some paste for your arm, it's where the sea has given you an infection," he tells me, and I look at my arm. It's tied up with a white bandage. I quickly move away from him and to the other side of the bed. The room spins as I do so.

"Here, have this," Chaz says as he picks something up off the small dresser by the bed, his bright-green eyes locking with mine.

"What is it?" I ask, looking at the small, black cup he tries to hand me.

"Water, what else?" he says with a tired smile.

"You're a pirate. Why would I trust it not to be poisoned?" I ask him. I watch him closely as he shakes his head at me. I don't know why, but I feel slightly guilty for asking him that. I know he must have looked after me, but I just feel . . . I feel scared, and it's not something I'm used to feeling.

"I'm not going to tell you what to do, changed one, but I suggest that not all rumours are true," Chaz tells me. I frown at that. It's well known that pirates do whatever they want. They own the waters, and they trade passage for food and treasure, but end up killing the ones who are careless enough to make a deal with them. They kill anyone they want and take what they want. Even the king trades food and gold with them, so they leave him alone.

Then again, the changed ones are meant to be all-powerful with the power to destroy the land and seas. I don't have an ounce of power, and I've been hidden all my life for nothing. I guess if they wanted me dead, I would be. I wonder if it was Chaz who pulled me out of the water.

I take the glass, and he nods at me, his eyes looking me over before he steps away. I drink it, discovering that it is water. I feel a little silly for reacting so badly to him.

"Rest, I will keep you safe," he tells me, his words soothing but protective. This pirate doesn't know me, so why would he speak to me so kindly. I look over at him in confusion. I don't get why they would save me from the water, why they would bother keeping me alive?

"Why?" I ask him.

"I may be a pirate, and you may be a changed one, but we are all still people. All people should know kindness, and I doubt you have had much of that in your life," he says, then walks away. I watch him pull a book off his desk and sit in the chair next to it to read.

"My name is Cassandra," I tell him as he takes his seat, his deep-brown eyes meet mine. I don't know why I told him my name, but I feel safe, if only for a second around him.

"Rest, Cassandra," he says softly, his words having the reaction he wants as I drift off to sleep, his deep-green eyes haunting my dreams.

7

CASSANDRA

The sound of a pencil scraping across paper wakes me up from my dreams of the sea and brown eyes. I move slightly, feeling that I'm still in bed and still smelling the strong herbs. My arm burns a little now, and I place my hand on it. It feels warm, but I don't know if that's a good thing. I move so I'm lying on my side, and so I can see the room. It's night now, and the room is lit by two candles in lanterns.

Chaz is leant over the desk, writing something quickly. I don't have many options, but I'm not senseless enough to stay on a pirate ship with a load of pirates I don't know. *I would have more chance of living in the sea.* If this pirate is being nice to me, there is every chance he wants me for some reason.

I have no intention of sticking around to find out what that reason is when I feel better.

I slide off the bed slowly, my feet touching the cold, wooden floor, and it creaks. Chaz lifts his head and his eyes meet mine.

"There is a toilet over there," he points to the door near his desk and turns back to his work. I smile internally as I spot the heavy-looking book next to my bed. I slide it into my hand and hide it behind my back as I walk over to him. I pause a little, feeling unsure about hurting him. It feels wrong. I force myself to remember all the stories about pirates that I've heard, the stories my father has told me, and I ignore how I feel.

I quickly whack him on the back of his head with the heavy book, and he slides off the chair landing in a heap on the floor. I drop the book, feeling more than a little guilt as sickness slides up my throat.

Never turn your back on a woman. I read that in a book somewhere, and it's apparently true. Men really underestimate us, and pirates are no exception to that rule.

"I would say sorry, but you're a pirate. I'm sure you have done worse," I say as I feel his pockets and pull out a key. I slide it into the door and pop my head into the corridor. The sound of water splashing against the boat and the distant noise of someone snoring can be heard. After a second of waiting, I pull the door closed behind me and lock it. Just in case.

The corridor is dark, with only two candles in wall sconces on the wall. There are boxes lining the corridor, perfect to hide behind as I make my way to the stairs at the end.

All these years of being hidden makes me great at being invisible, but there is no need. All the doors are shut that I pass, and there is no one around. I make it to the stairs and quickly run up them, hating every creak my feet make. At the top of the stairs are two flat doors, so I push one of them open and pop my head out, finding that I'm lucky as no one is around. I pull myself out of the door, shocked at how light it is, and shut it quietly behind me. When I turn around, it's to see I'm in the middle of the ship. Three big sails fill the skies, one is black with a white skull in the middle, the typical sign for pirates here. The wind is strong and blows cold, wet air into my face as the ship rocks against the waves. I can see the outline of the big wheel that steers the ship. The ship is made of shiny-looking dark wood, and I admit to myself that the ship is cleaner than I thought a pirate ship would be. The mast in the middle has little handles all around it, and ropes tied around them. There are ropes everywhere as I look around. *How can anyone know what they do?* There are two boats on one side of the ship, perfect for me to take one and escape. I don't know anything about ships, only little bits from books, but it's nothing like what I read. The books can't make you feel the gentle movement of the ship, the salty breeze, or the sound of the wind hitting the sails.

I stop, looking around, when I hear a clap and a laugh behind me.

I spin to see a male shadow leaning against the wooden wall where the captain's room must be. The man's laugh fills the night as he steps into the moonlight. He is tall, wearing a black pirate hat, and his hair is as black as the night, long and wavy as it falls to his chest. He has a blue feather braided into his hair on one side, and it moves in the wind. The pirate is wearing all black, with a long, black sword hanging from his belt. I narrow my eyes at his dark ones as he opens his arms and smirks.

"A nice night for a stroll," he says, his voice deep and seductive. I finally understand what the people wrote about in my books when they say a man's voice is seductive. His voice makes me want to walk to him, if it wasn't for the sarcasm I can pick up in his words.

I simply smile as I move my eyes away from him to the small boat hanging off the side of the boat. *If I can get there and—*

"Don't think about it," the man warns, his voice full of humour, and I snap my eyes to his.

"Try to stop me then." I laugh when his eyes widen, in shock or humour, I don't know. I quickly make a run for it. I don't even get close to the boat when I'm tackled to the deck. The man turns at the last second, so I land on him, his arms holding me tightly against him. I do the only thing Miss Drone told me to do to win in a fight against a man. I lift my knee and slam it up in between his legs. The man groans and yet doesn't let go as he rolls me over and pins me down on the cold, damp deck of the ship. The wind picks up strands of his hair, as bits of water splash against us from the harsh sea.

"You are a brave little bird, aren't you?" his deep tone says next to my ear.

The pirate has no idea.

"Get the hell off of me," I spit out and struggle to move as he laughs.

"Women don't usually say that when they are

under me, little bird," he says. I look up at him in disgust, which only seems to make him laugh more.

"They must be dumb as well as blind then," I grit out when he pushes his hard body into mine. I try to ignore how he feels so warm, and I feel that draw to him, like I did with Chaz.

"I'm going to like you," he says with a chuckle as he watches me.

"Hunter, the girl knocked Chaz out and has esca–" a man says and stops a few steps away from us.

"What in the seas are you doing on top of her?" the other man says, but I don't take my eyes off Hunter as he replies.

"Do you need a lesson in women, Jacob?" Hunter replies, keeping his body on top of me as he laughs, his dark blue eyes still watching mine the whole time.

"Apparently you do, Hunter, get off her," Jacob says, and Hunter does slowly, keeping his eyes on me. I push myself to my feet and take a step back. I glance over at this Jacob man; my first thought is that he is clearly another pirate. Jacob has light-brown hair which is slightly curly and slightly out of control. He has a full beard that looks soft, and he has a black pirate hat on, which has a white strip around it.

"Hear us out first. I didn't jump into the Green Sea after you to watch you kill yourself now, Cassandra," Jacob says, and I close my eyes, trying to reason with myself. I can't run, and I can't swim away from here. His warm, blue eyes watch me closely. I'm guessing that Chaz told Jacob my name.

I open my eyes just in time to see a big wave splash against the side of the boat and wonder if jumping without a boat is a good idea.

Would the Sea God save me?

8

CASSANDRA

"Why did you save me?" I ask Jacob, pulling my gaze away from the water. He and Hunter watch me carefully, all their muscles strained and tight, just like their stern faces. *Like they expect me to jump off the ship and swim away.* I can't say I'm not thinking of doing just that, because I'm not sure why they want me alive. I've heard stories of men that keep women, and I have no desire to be any part of their plans.

"Simple. I would never let someone die that I had the power to save," Jacob says, his voice soft and slightly kind. I look him over. His long, black coat stops around his knees, and the wind is blowing it harshly away from him. He is very good-looking for a pirate.

"Well, thank you, but I need to be going," I say and take a step towards the edge of the ship. The salty sea breeze fills my senses, and the night is lit up by the thousands of stars in the skies. It's a strange thing to see the stars from a different point of view. I look around the sea, but I can't see anything near, no islands to swim to. I have no idea which sea we are in or how far we are from any land.

"We have an offer," another man says, walking out of the captain's rooms. I watch as he comes into the light. The man is the spitting image of Hunter, so they must be twins. He has a purple feather braided in his long, black hair instead of Hunter's blue one. This man has his tied back by a bandana around his head, but it's shorter than Hunter's. He seems more commanding, but kinder, than his twin. Hunter seems to like scaring people, and I know that from the small amount of time we spoke together.

"What kind of offer?" I ask him. The others are still as I take another step back, but their eyes watch. I meet Hunter's eyes, and he smiles. A smile which tells me he finds me amusing.

"We are travelling to Fiaten, and we could take you with us. We offer places to people who need help. We will offer you food and safe travel," Jacob says, as the other man moves to stand next to him.

"Safe?" I laugh, and the other man narrows his eyes.

"I promise you that you will not be harmed," the man says, his light-blue eyes watching me closely, and I have to hold in the slight fear I feel in front of them all. They are intimidating, standing close to each other and completely still as they watch me. Based on the way they interact, I have no doubt that they are friends.

"Tell that to mister dark and scary over there." I point a finger at Hunter, who just smiles. It's creepy and yet, he has a really nice smile. I have to keep reminding myself that they are all pirates, because when I look them over, they look like the men out of the romance books I read. They're very handsome, and it makes me want to forget who they are.

Who I am.

"My brother will not harm you," the man says, his voice holding no argument.

"I make no promises, Ryland," Hunter says, his words slow and dark.

"Shut it, Hunter," Ryland snaps back, and they both stare at each other. My eyes meet Jacob's as I take another step back. My feet are now hitting the side of the boat.

"Even if I stay here, I'm a changed one. Anyone who sees me will try to kill me. I need to go somewhere off the charts, and that's not going to happen if you drop me off at a random port," I say, and three pairs of attractive eyes turn to stare at me.

"There is a place that is safe for your kind, and I will take you," Ryland tells me. I have the feeling he runs most of the ship; he has that boss-like attitude. I don't believe for a second there is a place safe for me. If there was, my father would have taken me there. Changed ones are never safe.

"I don't believe you,"

"There is nowhere else you can go, nowhere that is safe. We have had changed ones on board before and taken them to Fiaten. They will help you in the mountains," Ryland tells me.

"Why would they help changed ones? Why would they help me?" I ask.

"They can teach you, help you learn about who you are and what you can do. Don't you want to learn what it means to be a changed one?" Jacob says softly, and I hesitate a little. I don't know anything about who I am, and if they are right, I may find a way to keep myself safe. They might even know how I can get these powers they spoke of.

"What do you want in exchange for taking me there?" I ask, crossing my arms.

"Nothing," Ryland says.

"I can't and won't believe that. No one does something for nothing in this world," I say and turn around. I climb on to the side of the boat, holding the rope and look down at the sea. The waves look huge and frightening. A part of me accepts that I will die in these waters if I jump, and another part of me wants to stay on the ship to live.

"Then jump, little bird. See if you can fly," Hunter says, and I simply smile as I look over my shoulder at him.

"I'm taking the boat," I tell them, and Hunter laughs. Ryland just crosses his arms in annoyance, and Jacob looks up at the sky.

"Without saying hello to me?" a deep voice I recognise says to the left of me, where I can't see him. I turn sharply to face him as his sea-blue eyes smile up at me. The guy called Dante, who was at the party, moves to stand in front of me, looking far more like a pirate than he did when we met.

"You're a . . .," I get out, and he places his hands over my legs, locking me in place and stopping me from moving.

"A pirate, pretty girl, and you are not going anywhere."

9

CASSANDRA

"You can't lock me in here forever, you crazy, arrogant pirates!" I yell as I kick the door that the said pirates have locked after leaving me in here. Dante pulled me off the side of the boat, and I kicked him in between the legs in anger. I can't admit that it didn't feel great when he fell to the floor in shock. But then, Hunter threw me over his large shoulder and threw me in here. I glance around the room; it's the room I woke up in, but Chaz isn't here.

What are the chances of Dante being a pirate? The first guy I met other than my father, and he is a pirate?

The first man I have ever found attractive. I can't even say he is the last man I've found attractive; all the pirates are good-looking. When I think about it, I know that it's really unfair that I will need to become like my father and kill at least one of them to be able to escape. He wouldn't hesitate to kill one of them, to make sure they don't hurt me. I'm thinking that Hunter is the one I need to get rid of, because he is the most dangerous one. Only it's not me, I wouldn't know how to kill one of them and not have it haunt me. I just can't think how I'm going to get out of this any other way, and I just need to come up with a plan. I glance around the room, spotting that all the books on the desk are gone. There is nothing other than a chair that I could use to protect myself. Well truthfully, there is a pillow, but that is not going to be useful to me.

I walk over to the small window in the room and lift myself up on my tip toes, so I can see out of it. The night sky is lit by thousands of bright stars, and they look brighter out here than they did from my house. I wonder what my father is thinking now. I don't think he will look for me; my father may care somewhat for me, but his position on the council means a lot to him, too. No, I know I'm on my own now and the chances of seeing him ever again are low.

The turning of a key makes me jump, and I quickly run behind the door before it's opened. I lift the surprisingly heavy chair and hold it over my shoulder as the door opens. I swing it down on the back of the man coming into the room, but he lifts one hand and catches the chair. The man, who I haven't seen before, laughs. It's a deep, throaty laugh that is nice to hear.

"Now, now, little fighter, that was rude," the man says with a large grin. He has wavy, dark blond hair that's split in the middle and tucked behind his ears. The man's face is scarred on one side, with two deep gashes from his eyebrow down to his shaven chin. The red shirt and brown trousers he's wearing are covered by a massive belt, which has four daggers clipped in. He has large, leather gloves that stop at his elbows. I can see that his arms are muscular even under his clothes. When I finally look up, his dark green eyes are watching me closely. This man is older than the others and me. I would place him around twenty-five, but his eyes look older.

"Well, you shouldn't lock me up," I say, and he laughs as he pulls on the chair. I fall with it and smack into his chest, stumbling over my feet. He drops the chair and wraps an arm around my waist. I shiver, not used to anyone touching me, especially not a man. I force myself not to focus on how hard his chest feels pressed against mine.

"You have lovely eyes, my little fighter," the man says, his tone dropping deeper as I look up at him. At this angle, I can see how very attractive he is.

"I'm not your little anything," I grit out, and he grins.

"Not yet," he says before letting me go. I'm too flustered to reply to him as I take a step back. I don't know how to handle his comment, so I just decide to look away from him and forget it. *I hate how drawn I am to these damn pirates.*

They're pirates, and I have enough problems to worry about. I shouldn't be wasting my time thinking about them.

"Come on, and don't bother running," the man says and walks out of the room, leaving the door open. I'm too taken back to move as I look at the door. Did he really just leave me here with the door open? My only thought is how quickly I could run back to the little boat and get the hell out of here.

"Cassandra," the man says outside the door, and I sigh knowing that it was too easy. I quickly run my hand over my messy hair, feeling all the tangles and knowing I must look a mess. I walk out of the room after deciding that there's nothing to be done about it.

The man is leaning one shoulder against the wall of the corridor opposite the door when I come out. His gaze sweeps over my body as I stop in front of him.

"I forgot to say, I'm Zack," he says and moves off the wall. I watch as he walks down the corridor, not looking back once. My gaze drifts down the other direction of the corridor, to the stairs which I know lead above deck. I wonder if I can make it to stairs before Zack notices I'm gone. *Why would he leave me alone in the corridor to choose?*

No, it can't be that easy to escape.

I glance down to the way Zack has gone; there's a door open and light shines out of it. The noise of pots and pans banging can be heard, as well as the normal sounds of the boat creaking, and the whistle of the wind over the sea.

I don't know what makes me turn down the corridor and towards the open door, but I don't question it.

I can't.

I slowly pop my head around the open doorway. I don't really want to go in, but I'm curious. The room is a kitchen, with many wooden countertops and a pot hanging over a small fire. The fire is built on sand, which is inside a large metal container. There are ten or so barrels around the room. There are also boxes of what look like food piled on the sides.

The pirates have a lot of food by the looks of it. The people in my town would kill for this stuff.

I glance over at the pirate, Zack. I don't know what rattles me more, the fact that he isn't waiting for me to come in the room or how good-looking he is. I thought pirates where meant to have black teeth, and the scars on their faces are meant to be scary. Zack's just make him look more handsome. I move a little closer, so I can see that he's cutting up a yellow fruit I have never seen. I watch as he peels the skin off and cuts up the soft cream-coloured centre.

"What is that?" I ask, my voice softer than I wanted it to be.

"They are called bananas. I'm making you a toasted banana sandwich. It's my favourite," Zack says and doesn't look back at me as I walk over.

"Where do they grow?" I ask him as I stop next

to him. The only fruit we have ever had on Onaya was apples. The apple trees all died around five years ago when the rain didn't come for seven months. The council decided they couldn't waste the water on keeping the trees alive and started using sea water. All the trees died the morning after the water was poured on them. Everly told me that people believed the Sea God killed the trees in anger, because the council killed a baby that very morning. A changed one, a little boy. I wish the rumours were true, and the Sea God did decide to kill them all. Of course, the council still had apples. They had their own trees in their gardens, which they kept watered. My father had one, and I loved the apples there. I used to have one a week and give the rest to Everly. I really hope she and Miss Drone are doing okay on the island. I know losing her job would be difficult for them. They relied too much on the food my father gave them.

"Sevten. We trade a lot there, and these grow on the trees," he tells me. I wonder if I'll get to see any other islands. I spent so long looking at the maps of our world, wondering about what the islands actually look like.

"A lot of trees have died on Onaya," I tell him, trying to keep my eyes down on the wooden floor. I glance up as he nods at me. I watch him as he puts the cut-up banana pieces onto four slices of bread, and he puts them on a metal tray that rests over the pot.

"Some say the changed ones brought the rain and kept the land alive," he says, and I look at him in shock. I've never heard that one before. I know little of the supposed powers of the changed ones. I want to ask him more about what he has heard.

"Others say the changed ones have ruined the land, and we will all suffer," he says as he turns the sandwiches over with a spatula. My heart bangs against my chest, I have heard that one before. My father said the king told him it.

"Which do you believe?" I ask him, trying to keep my voice neutral.

He turns a little, so I can see his smile. "Neither," he says.

Zack takes the sandwiches off the tray and puts them on to two plates he has out. He offers me one, and I take it.

"You must be hungry," he says and opens a barrel. He pulls out an apple and offers me that as well.

"Here, I know Onaya once had lovely apples. These are green and not red, but they are still good," he says. I nod as I take the green apple off him, noticing how they are slightly rounder than the red apples we had. The apple may only be a small thing, but it reminds me of home, and it's sweet that he thought to get me it.

"Come," Zack turns with his plate and heads out into the corridor. He opens the door on the other side of the corridor. The room is lit by candles, so I can see it and it's empty. There's a long, wooden table, with dozens of chairs and pretty flowers in pots in the middle.

A pirate ship with flowers? Everly would never believe it if I told her. I guess I'll never be able to.

Zack takes a seat, and I take the one on the other side of the table, so I'm opposite him. I take a bite of the sandwich; the taste is so nice, and it's only seconds before I eat it all. I'm not used to much hot food, even at home.

"You're the cook?" I ask after we've eaten all of our food in silence.

"Yes. I was brought up on Sixa, and my parents were well-off. They were the richest in the town and both of them were on the council," he starts telling me. I remember reading about Sixa; the island is covered in snow and people are said to live in houses made from ice. There is also said to be massive creatures, completely white and dangerous that live there. I don't know how much of that is true, but the island is the smallest in our world.

"I used to cook food to give to the poor. When my family found out, they killed twenty people to stop me from helping them," he tells me, as he leans back in his chair. I'm surprised by how casually he tells me this, like it's just something he happens to know and not something that personally happened to him.

"Why would they do that?" I ask him, shocked that he would tell me this. It's shocking that he would tell me something so personal about his life. I'm not shocked that his parents killed that many people. They sound just like the council on Onaya, like my own father.

"I was in love with a poor girl. She was kind and yet, no match for my family. I was locked up while they killed her and all of her family," he tells me, and it's the first time I see any emotion on his face, but it's gone in seconds.

"I'm sorry," I say, and his bright green eyes meet mine.

"I killed them. Both of my parents. I paid for that and then escaped. The men you are running from saved my life," he tells me. I finally know why he told me this story of his life, for the ending. I don't want to admit how much I respect him for killing his parents after the terrible things they did. I could never do that to my own father, no matter how many people he killed. It must have been a horrible decision for him, but I'm guessing it was mainly done out of anger.

"You think I should trust them, trust you?" I ask, and he smiles.

"I believe you already do, my little fighter," he says, his words soft when he says that little nickname he calls me, and he stands up. I glance over his whole body, noting how big he is, how muscular. The long gloves and high neckline of his shirt hide most of his golden skin from me, and I wonder why he wears the gloves. It's warm in here, so it's not for that reason. I watch as he walks to the door.

"Go to sleep, and someone will show you around in the morning. You know the way to the room you woke up in," he says, and our eyes meet once more before he looks away.

I have to take a deep breath before I can say anything. "Wait," I say, and he stops in the doorway. "Is Chaz ok?" I ask quietly. I don't want to admit the guilt I feel for hurting him. I know I shouldn't want to know, but I do. *I need to know he is okay.*

"Only his ego has been bruised. I'm sure he would rather you didn't mention it," he says with a small, cheeky grin in my direction before he leaves.

10

ZACK

"So, what do you think of her?" Chaz asks when I lean back on my bed inside my room. Chaz is sitting on the desk by the door, sharping one of his daggers. I glance at my huge axe leaning against the wall, thinking that's it's been a long time since I've had any excuse to be in a fight and use it. The waters are calm, and most of the other pirates wouldn't be stupid enough to try to fight us. Our ship is one of the biggest in the water. The only ones who could battle against us would be the guard's ships, because their ships are the same size as ours. The king's ship is the largest in the seas, and no other ship would win a fight against it. I look over at Chaz, who is still watching me for my answer about Cassandra. I still remember the soaking-wet woman Jacob pulled out of the water. I watched as Chaz saved her life, breathing air into her lungs, and she coughed up a lot of green water. We all knew that it would be touch and go on whether she would wake up. Every one of us has watched her the last two days while she slept. She had a fever the first day, but once that passed, Chaz believed she would survive. I don't think any of us expected her to be so headstrong when she woke up. I knew she must have been hidden somewhere and I would guess her parents are high up, even on the council of Onaya. The only reason she would have run to the sea would have been because someone found out about her. That mark would have been a death sentence for her on that island.

"She is brave, smart, and beautiful. A very deadly combination with that mark on her forehead," I reply. Cassandra is all those things and more. I knew from the moment I met her dark eyes that matched the long, brown, soft-looking hair that she was different from any other woman I've met. The fact that she threw a chair at me when I walked in just made me laugh. She is brave, so brave to do that. It's surprising, as she couldn't have had much interaction with people, especially with men. Yet, the way she spoke to me earlier, you wouldn't think it. I knew she was scared, but she didn't show it. I like that about her.

"I know she's deadly. I got distracted by her beauty, too," Chaz huffs, and I laugh. Chaz is a good fighter; all my brothers on this ship are. They may not be related to me by blood, but we have spent three years fighting for each other and making sure we all stay alive. It's not easy when nearly every island has someone looking for us, for various reasons.

"She's also a small girl with no powers, who managed to knock you out with a book," I say, chuckling. Chaz narrows his eyes at me. I'm surprised she managed to knock him out cold with only a book. She must have some upper arm strength to do that. I wonder if she was taught to fight. I remember her small body, every part looks soft, and yet, her eyes blaze with a fire. A fire that tells you that you will get burnt if you get too close.

"Shut it," he says, making me laugh more.

"We need to keep her in one of our rooms until we get to Fiaten. I don't trust the men and women we have on board. You know as well as I that people act out of fear more than sense most of the time," I say. The people we have on board are getting off at our next stop, but they still can't be trusted. We may have helped them, but everyone fears the changed ones. They would fear her.

"Agreed. I will speak to Ryland about her sleeping in one of our rooms every night," Chaz says, looking down at the dagger and twirling it in circles. I don't like the idea of her sleeping in other guys' beds all the time, but there isn't much choice. We take it in turns to stay up at night and watch the ship, so she will always have an empty bed.

"I feel drawn to her, protective of her," Chaz says, surprising me. The strange thing is, I feel the same way. I haven't wanted to be close to any woman in years, so the feelings I get around Cassandra are strange to me.

"You are drawn to her as well," Chaz says after I don't reply. I am, more than I want to be. I would be of no use to a beautiful girl like her. I wouldn't ever push her for more than a friendship. My body is nothing to be admired after my punishment for killing my parents. I glance down at my glove-covered hands, knowing she would hate to see what they look like uncovered. *All the scars.*

"I know little of changed ones, but they are said to be kissed by the Sea God. Any beautiful woman kissed by a god would be easily drawn to. That's all it is," I say, and Chaz leans back in his seat, his eyes watching me too closely. He flips the dagger in the air and catches it, before repeating the motion.

"I don't believe it's just that. We should ask Ryland and Hunter about changed ones. There were many in their family, so if anyone knows anything, it would be them," he says.

"Yes," I nod. The twins' parents were changed ones, so they would be the ones to ask. The only problem is that they don't speak of their parents at all. They're running from them, like everyone on this ship is running from something. *Cassandra has more in common with us than she realises.*

"I have to go and check the ship," Chaz say, walking out of the room. I lie back on my bed, thinking about Cassandra and knowing that I won't be able to stop for a while.

She may never want me, but it doesn't mean I can't help her sort her life out and be her friend.

Just a friend.

11

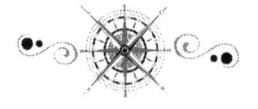

CASSANDRA

"Morning," a deep voice pulls me awake, and I lift my head from the comfy bed. I blink my eyes open to see Dante sitting on the desk on the other side of the room watching me. His clothes are similar to what he wore yesterday, but a different shirt; it's tighter, showing off his chest. His blue eyes shine, as the morning light fills the room. *His eyes really do look like the sea, so bright.*

"How long have you been in here?" I ask him as I sit up.

"Long enough to know you have a cute snore, pretty girl," he chuckles, and I feel my cheeks going red.

"That's creepy, pretty boy," I say with a little

grumble, and he laughs. I stretch my arms up, and my top rides up my thighs. I glance over at Dante who is fixated on the little part of skin that he saw, and he clears his throat, looking away.

"Breakfast is nearly ready, and I'm sure you will want to clean up. There are only three women on board and none of them are your size. So, we got the best we could," he says. *I wonder if one of the women on board is his wife.*

One of them must have a long-term partner on board or a girlfriend. They are very attractive pirates, and I bet they have their choice of women. I can't see Zack having one, considering he's on the run from the people of Sixa.

"Thanks," I say, and he nods before he slides off the desk. I see the long sword on his back as he walks to the door. The blade is a strange green in colour, not silver like I have seen other swords. It's massive and wide for a sword, too. I imagine it must be heavy, and it's in a leather holder on his back, the handle is a dark green metal, too.

"See you in a minute, pretty girl," Dante says.

"I have a name. It's Cassandra," I tell him, ignoring the flutter in my belly every time he calls me that.

"So do I, but everyone calls me it. I think you

are going to be special," he says and leaves me with red cheeks as I watch him shut the door.

Why do these pirates make me so flustered?

I stand up on the cold, wooden floor, resisting the urge to climb back into the warm bed. The room is so much colder than I'm used to. Onaya is warm nearly all year, so it was never cold when I woke up. This room is cold, and it's strange to get used to the rocking of the ship. I walk over to the desk, seeing the pile of clothes. The clothes turn out to be a very long, white shirt with buttons down the middle, and black trousers that look a little better, but look big. I can pull them up over my stomach and tie them with the laces. I pick up the clothes and look around the room for a bathroom.

There's a small door on the other side of the room, and I open it to find a box with a hole in it on the left. I've read about these, they have a tube that goes out the side of the boat and the bucket of water on the floor next to it is for pouring down it to push it out to sea. We have something similar at home but there is a lever to push water down that comes from the sea.

I use the toilet while I look at the other side of the room, there's a small glass-enclosed unit with holes in the floor. I glance up to see there's a metal circle unit above it and I'm guessing the switch on the wall turns it on to let water out. There are also a few wooden shelves with soaps and shampoos in glass bottles by the door. Underneath it are piles of neatly-folded towels. The bottles are tied to the wall with little pieces of string. I'm guessing that's to stop them falling in bad weather. It's actually quite smart. It's not too far from what I had at home. I undo the bandage and leave it on the side. I brace myself after I pull all my clothes off and pull the switch. Cold water falls from the little holes, only in little amounts, but I soon manage to quickly clean up and wash my hair. I dry myself with one of the towels I find on the shelf, and I'm surprised by how soft the towel is. We could never get them this soft on Onaya. I pull the clothes on after redoing my bandage, annoyed to find the shirt may be long but the first three buttons are missing. My breasts are now easy to see, but I don't have large ones, so it's not too bad. The trousers tie up nicely, and I pull on my flat shoes by the bed.

I find a small hair tie on the dresser by the bed, which I use to tie my hair up. I leave out the feather that's braided and tuck it behind my ear. Once I drink the water on the table, I move towards the door. I open it up and walk out, the loud sound of people laughing and dishes being moved coming from the kitchen and dining area. I mutter to myself about not being scared before moving my feet. *I can do this.*

I walk down the corridor. The door to the dining room is open. When I walk in, it's packed. The whole table is full of people I haven't seen. Hunter and Ryland are sitting in the middle, and an older lady with long, grey hair sits next to Hunter. Her eyes meet mine. She stands, and the room goes silent,

"You knocked out one of my boys?" she says in a crackly voice.

"Yes," I reply and cross my arms. I'm not going to say sorry for it, not to anyone other than Chaz. I resist the urge to look for him as the older woman stares at me. Even in her old age, you can tell she was once very beautiful.

"I like her," she says, and her crackly tone fills the room. "I am Laura and the boss of this ship. Sit down," she orders, and a few people laugh in the room. Ryland's laugh is loud, and I hold in a chuckle when Laura hits him on the back of the head with a large, wooden walking stick. *For a small old lady, she can move fast.*

"You and that damn stick," he says as she sits back down. Apparently, she doesn't care.

"Here," Jacob's voice comes from next to me, and he holds a seat out for me to sit in.

The room is still silent as I take the seat and mutter out, "Thank you."

I glance around the table; all the guys and Laura are sitting in the middle of the table. The only one who isn't here is Chaz. On the left side of the table are four men, all of them a lot older than me and eating their food. They don't look my way, but my gaze goes to the pretty woman sitting next to Ryland. She meets my eyes briefly before looking away. I know that look; she's scared of me.

The other side of the table has two women and to my surprise, three children. The children all look under ten, and they smile at me.

What an odd group of pirates.

The table has a lot of food I have never seen on plates in the middle. Most of them are fruits and vegetables. There are two large bowls with porridge in them. At least I recognise that and the bread. The purple, pink, and yellow fruits are new to me. I do see the bananas that Zack made me last night, and I see some apples.

"Eat up, and then we are having a little chat with you," Dante says, making my eyes drift to him. He is sitting on the other side of me, and he starts eating straight away as I watch him. Everyone carries on with their food as I sit in silence watching them. It's not an awkward silence, they just seem to be comfortable with each other. I try to catch the pretty woman's eyes but she doesn't look up. I do catch one of the other men's eyes, and he nods at me.

"Did you sleep well?" Jacob asks from my other side.

"Yes, thank you," I reply, keeping my tone neutral. I don't want to be nice, but I can't be mean to him. *This pirate saved my life.*

"Good," he says and smiles a little at me. I look away as Dante fills my plate with porridge. Ryland picks an apple up and places it next to my plate.

"Thanks," I mutter, and he nods. This is weird, and I'm not sure what else to say to them. The table goes back to talking once I start eating. I listen to their conversations about things I don't understand. Mainly about the running of the ship and how close they are to Sevten. The children giggle as they throw a ball between them and one of the mothers tells them off. *It's so...normal.*

Once I'm finished, Ryland stands up. The room goes silent, and I put down my spoon.

"Out," he says, and everyone hurries out other than the boys. Laura doesn't move until Ryland stares down at her. She huffs at him, but does get up and leaves. Laura's eyes meet mine for a second, and all I can see is worry. I have no idea why she would be worried for me, but she is.

Once the door shuts behind her, Ryland sits back down and leans back in his chair as I turn to watch him. The purple feather looks brighter in the daytime—against his black hair and black clothes. Ryland has this stern approach to him, which looks far more frightening when he leans forward and places his head on his joined hands. I feel like I have nowhere else to look as he speaks, other than to stare into his blue eyes.

"We have an offer," he says, his words slow as he looks at me. I see his eyes drop down my body slowly before he looks back up. I can feel my cheeks burning red, and I force myself to keep my eyes locked on his.

"I do as well," I say, and he raises an eyebrow.

"Do tell," he offers as a reply, a small, crooked smile appearing on his face.

"I will stay on board, *for now*, and I can cook and

clean for you. I'm sure I can find ways to help you if you don't need those. When we stop off next, I will leave," I say, and Ryland smiles, his gaze switching to Zack, who nods at me with a little wink.

"Zack does need some help in kitchen," Ryland offers, and I nod.

"So, everything is agreed," I say as I stand up, wanting to get away from all the attractive eyes on me.

"Not quite. We will be stopping off at Sevten first, and you will need to be hidden. Then we are travelling to Fiaten, where you can leave if you wish," he tells me. That's a long journey with them. If we are traveling to Sevten now, then we must be in the Middle Sea. I know enough from the maps to know the middle sea is one of the biggest and known for the number of pirates that travel the waters.

"Why can't I just get off at Sevten?" I ask. Everly has travelled to the very top of Onaya, but she says you can't do much when you get to that side as it's much higher. There is a big cliff on Onaya that looks over the Middle Sea. Everly said it's a blue water with a slightly green tone to it, but the skies are clear, making it easy to travel on.

"On the islands, changed ones are killed as

babies, and Sevten has a slightly different rule." Hunter says bluntly, and I look at him with a clear unspoken question. *What could they possibly do with changed ones other than kill them?*

"On Sevten, they are sold to the highest bidder. Changed ones are worth a fortune, a fortune many people would kill for. There is a price on your head, a very big one. I haven't seen or heard of a female changed one in years," Hunter tells me. I don't get it, surely there must have been other girls with my mark born. I look around at all of the guys, wondering what's stopping them from selling me.

"How do I know you won't sell me?" I ask, stepping back from the table. They may have pulled me out of the sea, just to find out they have a big treasure to sell. It would make sense why they went to so much effort to keep me on board. Hunter keeps his dark eyes locked on mine, making me realise that even if he looks just like his brother, his eyes give him away. I don't even have to look at the feather in his hair to know it's Hunter; those dark eyes have such depth to them. Such hate. I don't think the hate is for me, but it's there.

"Never trust a pirate, little bird," Hunter says with a slow grin. I grin back at him, which seems to make him a little concerned. *The pirate should be worried.*

"I prefer the saying, always kill a pirate." I say just as slowly, and he smirks at me as his eyes drop gradually, looking at every part of my body. It's like he's just realising I'm a woman or something. I can't say I mind the attention from Hunter, though. He seems to draw me in with his snarky words and passion-filled looks.

"Enough!" Ryland slams his hand on the table, making me look away from Hunter.

"You need to learn to trust someone, and I will prove that you can trust us in a week's time when we arrive on Sevten. We will keep you safe and fed. There are few other pirates in these waters who will offer you the same deal. So, if you want to leave, then fine, we will not stop you, but it would be a foolish decision," Ryland says and storms out of the room.

"Impressive. No one ever gets a reaction out of Ry," Dante comments into the silent room. I watch the door closely, wondering if I should go after him. I don't know him, but I feel like he's right. There are few people that would offer me the same kind of safe passage that they are.

"Should I go and talk to him?" I eventually ask.

"No. Ry is just worried about you and doesn't show it well," Jacob answers my question.

"Why would he be worried about me?" I ask.

"Ry thinks it's his job to keep everyone alive who is on this ship. We all know you would be dead if you left now. None of the local islands can be trusted, and you would never get to Fiaten without a big ship to travel on. We may be pirates, we may have killed a lot of people, and we may not have the best morals, but . . .,"

"But what?" I ask gently.

"But, we will keep you safe if you let us, Cassandra," he says, his voice softer than mine.

"Okay," I find myself saying, watching Jacob closely. I don't know why, but these pirates make me feel safe. Safer than I have ever felt, and it's concerning. I really don't believe they are planning to hurt me. They would have done so by now if they needed to. Jacob nods once before he looks down and walks out.

"Don't worry, you can trust us," Zack says to me before he walks out. Hunter and Jacob follow after him, leaving me alone with Dante.

"I'm your tour guide, but first, how's your arm?" Dante asks me.

"It's fine. I took the bandage off to have a look,

and it's only a little sore. I wrapped it up again," I tell him, being honest.

"It isn't bleeding?" he asks, coming over and lifting my arm. I'm surprised he remembered which arm it was, but he turns my arm a little and seems happy with the lack of blood on the shirt.

"It wasn't that bad of a cut," I say.

"Still. I don't want you in pain," Dante responds, and I finally notice how close he's standing.

"So, you're showing me around?" I ask.

"Come on, pretty girl. It's about time you learn how to live on a ship," he says and links our fingers before we walk out.

Learning about a ship is the last thing on my mind. I need to learn how to protect my heart from these pirates.

12

CASSANDRA

"So, this is the deck," Dante waves a hand over the deck of ship. The men I saw at breakfast are running around, and two of the children are sitting on the benches reading old-looking books. The men glance my way, but they seem to be busy. The woman I saw at breakfast is polishing the wood by the two glass doors that must lead to the captain's rooms. I can't see anything but ocean for miles out here as I glance around, and it's strange to be so far from land. The ocean seems calm, and some part of me, only a little bit, feels strangely happy here. *I always wanted to be close to the sea.* The stories Everly told me were not close enough to make me understand what it's like, they weren't enough. There is nothing like this, the smell of the sea, the breeze pushing small strands of my hair all over my face. The ocean air smells like salt, and the salty water can be tasted in the wind. I glance up at Dante, who is watching me closely but letting me silently take it all in. I just smile, and he runs his hand through his curly, brown hair with his own small smile. *I wonder if he likes the ocean as much as me.*

The ship has three large, black sails, and a mixture of smaller ones on the sides of the large one. The largest flag has a skull on it, with bones crossed behind the skull. At the helm of the ship, I can see Hunter behind the large circular wheel. Hunter looks every bit the pirate out of my books, with a black bandana around his hair and forehead. The blue feather is the only colour on him, and his long black coat seems to stand still against the wind. I watch as he turns the wheel slightly to the left, and when he looks my way, I turn to look at the ocean, so he doesn't see me looking at him. The ocean is all you can see for miles; the deep, blue sea and bright sun in the sky, yet it doesn't feel warm out here. I hold my arms around myself a little closer, as it's freezing out here.

"Here," Dante says as he takes his large, black cloak off and wraps it around my shoulders. It smells like him, just like the sea. I remember wondering what he smelled like when I first met him, and now I realise it's just the sea. The very sea he lives on. Dante's hands slide down my arms as he lets go of the coat, and we both just stare at each other. We are too close; my heart is pounding too fast, and his lips look too nice. I've never been kissed, not once, but the thought of kissing Dante is going through my mind. I don't know why I'm so drawn to him. *To them all.* Dante seems to see something in my gaze, because he lets go of my arms.

"So, what is the ship called?" I ask as he moves away.

"The Crimson Mermaid," he tells me, and I smile.

"I read a book once about mermaids, well the fantasy of them," I say. I always thought they were such unusual creatures. The mermaids are said to be half human and half fish. They are also said to have voices so sweet that you can do nothing but walk straight to them while they lure you into a sweet death. They live in water, so that would be walking straight into a death for any human. My father always told me that mermaids were just fairy-tales.

"Maybe they are not all fantasy," he winks at me, and I surprise myself by laughing.

"Mermaids are not real," I say, shaking my head.

"How would you know?" he asks me and then takes my hand. His hand feels rough in mine, like he uses his hands a lot. I guess I wouldn't know, I only have my books as knowledge, and there's a chance he might know the answer.

"Do you know?" I ask. I'm sure my eyes look wide in shock as I stare up at him.

"Yes, but I'm not telling you the answer. You have to earn it," he says, and I laugh again.

"How do I earn that answer?" I ask.

"I'll let you know, but I would take a kiss in exchange," he says as he winks at me, and I just laugh. *The pirate is cheeky, I will give him that.*

"So, over here are the captain's rooms, well Ryland's rooms," he tells me as he points to the glass, double doors.

"There isn't much more to show you up here. Let's go below deck," he says.

Dante leads me to the doors we came from and opens them up. I walk down, and he follows, closing the doors behind him. I let him take my hand when we get to the bottom of the stairs, and he walks us down the corridor.

"So, all of our rooms are on this corridor. You slept in Chaz's room last night. He's the ship doctor, if you didn't already guess that," he tells me. I feel even worse for hitting him now that I know he was the one that must have looked after me. I also know why that bed smelled so nice. It was Chaz's bed, and it must have smelled like him. My mind flashes to the pirate in question, and I remember his soft, blond hair and light-brown eyes. The pirate doctor was extremely attractive, and I hit him on the head with a book.

"This is mine, and that's Hunter's room," he points to the two doors opposite each other.

"Those are Jacob and Zack's rooms," he says when we move down the corridor and stop at two more doors. We carry on walking down the corridor, past the kitchen and dining room, and I see4

554 another set of stairs.

"Down here are the rooms our guests use, and storage," he says but doesn't take us down there.

"So, I'll sleep down there," I say.

He stops me from walking down by pulling on my arm gently, "No, you can sleep in one of our rooms. We take turns staying up at night to watch the ship, so one of our rooms is always free."

I move away from him in shock. "I can't do that," I say, shaking my head, my cheeks going red.

Dante moves closer and places his hand on my cheek.

"You are so lovely when you blush, pretty girl," he says, and I don't know why, but my anger disappears into laughter.

"You are such a flirt, pretty boy," I say through my laugh, and he only moves closer. The simple step tells me he isn't joking around with me, and my laugh disappears as I look up at him. Every part of me is drawn to him, wanting to be closer, and I find myself leaning into his touch slightly.

"Dante!" a man shouts down the corridor, making me jump back as we break apart. Dante shakes his head, watching me for something.

"There will be a time where we won't always be interrupted," Dante whispers just for me as the man who shouted runs down the corridor.

"Ryland wants you," the man says. The man is young, more a boy than a man, as I would guess he is around fifteen. He has a slightly spotty, pale face under a large hat, and his clothes are baggy on his thin frame.

"Roger, this is Cassandra," Dante introduces us, and Roger bows low. I try to hide my smile, wondering why he is bowing to me. *I'm certainly not any princess or queen.*

"Hi," I say, and he meets my gaze with a smile. I'm surprised, not used to seeing no fear when people look at me. Roger doesn't even glance at my mark, which is a welcome relief.

"Roger is a permanent member of our ship," Dante tells me. "I'd best go and see what Ry wants. Zack is in the kitchens. So, you'd best go and see what he needs you to do," Dante walks away, his hand leaving mine slowly before he has to let go.

"You forgot your coat," I shout down the corridor to him.

"Keep it, it looks better on you," Dante says, but he doesn't turn around. Roger scurries after him after bowing for me one more time. *I will have to tell him that he doesn't have to do that.*

I follow them down the corridor and stop at the kitchens. The sound of light humming drifts from the dining room, and I turn my head to look around the open door.

Chaz is leaning over a book, humming away a soft song I have never heard. Music was not something my father liked in the house. I used to like to sing, until a man heard me once and came to the house. I was in the garden, and he was walking back from work I had guessed. I ran back to the house, but the man was stupid. He followed me and started shouting about me being a changed one when he saw my mark.

My father killed him as I hid in the kitchens with my hands over my ears. I will always remember coming out into the garden, just to see my father kick the dead body of the man into a hole he had dug up.

I chose not to sing a word since.

"Should I hide the books?" Chaz says suddenly, and I find I miss the sound of his singing. Chaz has had a haircut since the last time I saw him. His hair is now short, and it suits him more. I feel a little more trickle of guilt that he might have cut his hair off because I hit him on the head with the book.

"I'm sorry about that," I say quietly, and he smiles. Chaz has on a red shirt and tight trousers. The shirt is loose around his chest, and I can see the necklace he had on yesterday. Now that I'm closer, I can see all the shells are different, and there are seven of them. I wonder if there is one for each island and why he wears them.

"I knew your pretty smile was a knock-out, but I

can't say I expected to literally be knocked out by you," he says, and I laugh.

"Well, I am sorry about the whole hitting-you-on-the-head-with-a-book thing. I haven't met many people before, and I was scared," I tell him, being the most honest I think I can be. Chaz doesn't say anything as he closes the book and leans back in his chair. I let him silently watch me, before he decides to speak.

"I understand. Where did you grow up?" he asks me. I guess I could decide not to tell him, I guess I could walk off this ship, but I don't. *My heart and mind want to stay.*

"In my father's home," I say vaguely.

"I thought hitting me on the head with a book was our bonding moment, that you might start to trust me," he says with a smile, and it makes me chuckle with him.

"Sorry, it's just—" I start and find I don't know how to explain why I'm still being secretive with them.

"How about I guess a few things about you and you can tell me if I'm right?" Chaz asks. I'm curious to know how many things he could guess. It would give me a good idea about how smart he is.

"You can try," I say as I lean against the open door.

"Your father was part of Onaya council," he says straight away.

"How did you . . .?" I ask.

"Easy. When you met Dante, I was there. I was the one who called him over, and I saw you. Your dress was expensive, the face paint to hide your mark would not have been cheap, either. Also, you managed to get a boat and escape to the sea, which only the rich could do," he says, and he is right. No one could afford a boat in our town, and no one would have the money for the face paint unless they were well-off. The only reason I survived as long as I did was because of my father's money and power.

I nod, and he continues, "You don't trust people, because you have met so few, and you don't understand life well enough to trust it. As far as you're concerned, you were hidden and hunted by people for a simple mark on your forehead. A mark that does nothing," he says, explaining me with words I don't have. I'm surprised that he knows my mark does nothing, and I wonder if he knows of any way for me to tap into my powers.

"You're right. I only knew three people in my life. My father, my best friend Everly, and her mother who taught me everything I know. My father was on the council," I tell him, and he smiles gently.

"Being around men, it is different for you," he says, and I only nod as a response. It's worse, because I have no women to talk about my feelings to. *Is it normal to have crushes on six pirates?* Every single one of them is very attractive, and I've been so sheltered in my life, that this is confusing to me.

"Cassandra, you are far stronger than most, and you don't have to hide here. That I can promise you. No one on this ship will condemn you for a mark," he says, and I cross my arms.

"I do have to hide. I will always have to hide from the world, just so I can survive. The king has a price on my head, and the powers I am meant to have, I don't," I tell him. I'm not annoyed or angry at him, but I know my tone comes across that way. The world has given me nothing but a life full of hiding, a Sea God that doesn't exist, and a king that hunts my kind.

"No, you don't, and you will realise this soon. Live, Cassandra, or what is the point of all this hiding? You are finally free," Chaz says and stands up.

"I don't feel very free, Chaz," I say softly.

"You are. Cassandra, you are freer than most and more special than you know. It also helps that you are building friendships with pirates who are known to be protective of their own," Chaz says and picks up his book. He stops right in front of me, only a breath away as I process his words. *Would the pirates protect me? I can't see it.*

"Say my name again," Chaz asks me softly.

"Chaz?" I say, mimicking his soft tone, and he closes his eyes.

"My name sounds beautiful on your lips, just like their owner," he says with a small smile, and I take a deep breath, feeling a fluttering in my stomach as his eyes meet mine.

"Live, Cassandra," he says softly and leaves.

My name sounds even more beautiful on his lips.

13

CASSANDRA

"Very good," Zack compliments me after I finish washing up all the dishes from lunch. The meal was surprisingly quiet, and I learned that three times a day, they sit down to have a meal. Three meals a day is a lot, and it's hard to get my head around how much food they have. They don't waste food, though. They always manage to eat all the cooked food, and I helped Zack put back the extra food. In some ways, it makes that bit easier to accept. They all spoke to me a little over the meals, and they mainly asked about Onaya. I was thankful they seemed to stay away from asking about my family or the mark.

"That barrel is moving." I point a finger at one

of the barrels which is shaking from side to side. *I really hope they don't have rats here.*

Zack stomps over and pulls the lid open, reaches in and pulls out a big red cat. The cat is huge, with a large stomach and bright-red fur. I've heard of cats and seen drawings of them in books, but there weren't any on the islands. The cat meows loudly and starts hissing. *I wouldn't say it is friendly at all, but very handsome for a cat.*

"Salty Sam, how many times have I thrown you off this ship, and you keep coming back?" Zack says, and the cat meows again as he swipes a paw at him, catching his shirt. Zack puts him down on the floor, and he runs out of the room. Zack mutters a few things under his breath as he looks down at the scratch holes in his black shirt.

"Salty Sam?" I ask with a small smile, Zack just laughs.

"I thought we had left that cat on Sevten the last time we were there," Zack says and shakes his head.

"How did he get back on board?" I ask him, sucking in a breath when Zack pulls his shirt off. Zack's chest is muscular on the top, and his stomach is flat, with toned muscles dipping down into his trousers. He doesn't notice my staring as he pulls a drawer open and gets out a small metal box. When he turns around, I hold in my gasp. Zack has scars all over his back. They must have been so painful and look as if all have been done with a whip. Zack turns to look at me, his eyes watching me closely, and I don't say a word. I know that must have been the punishment for killing his parents.

"Don't ask. That cat appears everywhere, and is always eating the food," he says, quickly changing he subject, and I laugh a little, but my laugh dies off as I look at all the barrels.

"There are so many starving people on Onaya," I say, and he nods as he sits on one of the barrels. I watch as he opens the small box and pulls out a needle and some string. I watch him closely, wondering if he will take the gloves off to use them.

"You met Dante on Onaya, right?" he asks me as he threads the string through the needle perfectly, even with his gloves on.

"Yes," I say.

"I was with him and Chaz. We had just given ten barrels of food to the orphanage. Onaya is worse off than a lot of the islands, so we try to help," he tells me. I wondered what Dante was doing on the island, and now that I think back to it, it makes sense. There was no need for them to be on the island. *These pirates just keep shocking me.* I look back at the barrels of food as Zack stitches his shirt back together. All the things I've been told about pirates are coming back to me.

The seas are lost, pirates are death.

Always kill a pirate.

Pirates rule the sea and don't welcome strangers.

Pirates have black teeth and evil eyes from the deaths they have caused.

These are all the things I've been told more than once in my life. Yet, every one of them is untrue for these pirates.

"Maybe you should go for a walk," he says, nodding a head towards the door. I know Zack suggests this because I've stood staring at the dozens of barrels of food for way too long, and I look back at him; my eyes travelling over every part of his skin I can see. There aren't any scars on the front of his chest or his upper arms. Only a lot of muscle and smooth, tanned skin. When I look up to his face, it's to see him staring at me.

"You're a very handsome pirate," I say, then grin at him when he looks at me in shock. *I don't think he expected me to say that.* I didn't expect me to say that, either, but it's true. Zack is very handsome. I turn and walk out of the kitchen, feeling my back burning with his gaze, but I don't turn to look. I walk down the corridor, not seeing anyone else and loving the noise of the ship. Growing up in a silent house and everything being so quiet was never something I liked. I like the noise, and the sound of the ship as it sails through the ocean is soothing in a way. I quickly run up the stairs leading to the outside of the ship, wanting to see the ocean.

I bump into a woman when I step outside the doors to the deck. She tumbles over, and I quickly reach a hand to pick her up.

"Don't touch me," she screeches and scurries across the wet floor to get away from me. I recognise her as the woman sitting by Ryland last night. The woman has long, brown hair, in a complicated plait. I would place her as a little older than me. Her blue eyes watch me in fear.

"I'm not going to hurt you," I say, and she gets up on her own. She just stands there as the ship rocks from the waves, and she stares at my mark. I don't know what she is going to do, but I simply watch.

I hear laughing, and I turn to look at the man. I find Hunter leaning against the main mast of the ship. It's annoying to see his smirk as I glare at him. *I didn't even notice him there.*

"No, the changed one is just here to sprinkle

flowers and happiness on the ship. Don't run from her or you might hurt her feelings. Then everything could go boom," Hunter says and makes a show of doing a big clap with his hands. The woman's eyes widen in fear and she runs away, straight to the stairs that are next to me. She moves so slow next to me, and I go to say something but decide against it. Anything I can say to her will just scare her more. So, I just take a step back, and she quickly goes down the stairs and pulls the door shut.

"Why did you do that?" I ask, turning to Hunter. My tone is sharp and annoyed.

"I was only informing the poor woman about you," he says with a dark chuckle.

"What do you care, anyway?" I ask, putting my hands on my hips.

"Nothing, little bird. I care nothing about changed ones," he sneers out, and I glare at him as I walk away. I walk straight towards the glass doors that lead to the captain's room. I just want to get away from him and hopefully someone else will be in there.

"Little bird," Hunter says, and I turn to see him standing only a step away from me.

"Get lost, Hunter. Don't you have someone else to be cruel to?" I say, crossing my arms. Hunter just laughs darkly as he walks over to me, I walk backwards until my back is pressed against the cold, glass doors of the captain's room. He stops right in front of me, close enough that I can feel the warmth of his body. I lift my head to stare into his eyes, debating kicking him again, but instead, I can't stop looking at his eyes. Hunter has dark blue eyes, like a dark, stormy night. It's a weird shade of the darkest blue that almost seems a dark grey. So dark and enchanting. *Much like his personality.*

"Why haven't you run?" he asks me after a moment's silence. I'm surprised that his words are soft, unlike every other time he has spoken to me. I begin to answer when the door is opened behind me, and I fall backwards. Hunter goes to catch me, but just misses, and I slam onto the floor. I blink my eyes open to see Ryland looking down at me with a confused expression. He offers his hand, and I let him pull me up.

"You alright?" he asks me.

"Yes, I was just talking to–" I say, turning to see Hunter, but the space where he was is now empty. Hunter has left me here, and I'm not even a little bit surprised.

14

CASSANDRA

"Doesn't matter," I say to Ryland with a shake of my head, only after staring at the empty space where Hunter was for a long time. It doesn't surprise me that Hunter just walked off. I just can't understand why he would talk to me so softly, like he actually cared.

"Why don't you come in?" Ryland asks me, but doesn't wait for an answer as he walks back into the room. I shut the doors behind me, looking at the stained glass. The glass is a mixture of oranges and reds blended together. It looks like a sunset, and is very lovely. I turn and walk into the room, stopping to look around. The room is larger than I would have expected from the outside. There is a bed tucked into the one side and a massive, wooden table in the middle. The wall near the bed is full of shelves, with books piled on them. The table is full of things, everything from maps to gold cups and jars of random things. The walls are red in here, and there's a big window where I can see blue sea for miles. There isn't a cloud in the blue skies, and in the far distance, I can see two ships. When I look closer, I can see their black sails. *More pirates.*

I walk over to the window and stare out at the sea and the ships. I can feel Ryland's eyes on me, but it's such a gorgeous view. The sea is so beautiful, and I'm guessing it's the Middle Sea, because it's not green. It's a deep-blue that sparkles as the bright sunlight hits it.

"Must be strange to see the sea," he comments as he moves to stand next to me. We both just stare at the ocean for a while, watching as birds fly through the skies.

"Very," I reply. It is very strange, but somehow, it feels right. *I feel more at home on this ship than I ever did in my home.*

"The king will be looking for you by now. He was expected at your island two days after you ran," Ryland tells me and steps away. He doesn't have to tell me what I already know. I know the king will send the guards after me, and the last place I want to be is with the king. I'm sure he would make a spectacle of killing me, to warn others and make me out to be dangerous. I turn and watch as Ryland goes over to the big table and picks up an aged scroll. He unrolls the scroll out on the table and leaves glass paper weights on the corners. When I look around, I see the massive sword in a holder by the side of his bed. The silver sword handle catches the light and I wonder how he manages to lift such a heavy looking sword. *What is with these pirates and big swords?*

"Come here, Cassandra," he says softly. I walk over and stand next to him as I look down at the map. It's of our world, all the seven islands and the seven seas. It's a very detailed map, with each island showing their elements. Even the seas have drawings on them, from tornados for the Storm Sea and shipwrecks for the Lost Sea.

"What is this line?" I ask him. There's a black line connecting all the islands and little dates written next to each island. There is no year on the dates, just months.

"That's the route the king takes and the months he visits each island. You see, he is at Onaya now, and that is his last place before he returns home to Foten," he says as I run my finger across it.

Ryland takes my finger and moves it across the map to another set of lines. His hand feels rough and warm as it holds mine. I glance at our hands and then up to Ryland. He is really handsome; his features are more rugged than his brother's, and there's a certain feeling of power that comes from him. *I wonder what his story is. How did he become a pirate who runs a ship?*

"This is where the guards patrol. They will be at Sevten when we are there, for the auctions," he says and lets go of my hand. I glance down at the purple line he has shown me. It's a slightly different route from the king's, but he is right, it looks like the guards will be in Sevten this month.

"Auctions?" I ask. I have never heard of any auctions, but then I know little of Sevten. My books only told stories of the shape of the land and the weather.

"Not everyone is free. The auctions sell poor people to the richer families, and sometimes they sell a changed baby," he tells me. I move my hand away from the map to look at him.

"Why buy a changed baby to only have the king send his guards to kill them?" I ask. My tone is sharp, but it's not directed at him. I hate speaking about the deaths of the people like me.

They never have a chance to live because of the king.

"The only people who win the changed babies are guards, Cassandra," he says softly. Ryland moves closer and places his hand on my arm. His thumbs running soothing circles as I look at the map in anger.

"So they can kill them?" I snap out, pulling my arm away and walking over to the window. *I don't want to be soothed.*

"Yes. It's a perfect way to make sure all the changed ones are given to the guards. The auctions offer them money or food in exchange for the child. Most people would give up anything for either of those. I'm honestly surprised your mother or father didn't," he tells me. I don't look at him as I stare out the window. I wonder if my father knew of these auctions, and I wonder if he would have always kept me a secret.

"Why did you show me this?" I ask him, choosing not to comment on the mention of my father and why he hid me. I don't want to tell him about my mother and her death. I find it hard to speak to anyone about my mother. I don't move as he comes to stand right next to me, his arm pushed against mine.

"I'm not sure," he says, looking down at me. Ryland's eyes trace every part of my face before he leans forward, getting a wayward piece of my hair and tucking it behind my ear. I watch as he looks up from my eyes to the mark on my forehead and suddenly pulls away. Ryland walks over to the table, his back to me, but he looks very tense. I feel the same way as he does. *I'm too drawn to these pirates.*

"How do you know all this? Where the king will be?" I ask him. My father said no one knows what routes the king and his guards take so that they can't be attacked. This kind of information would be priceless to the people who hate the crown.

"Let's just say I know the king and queen well. I grew up in the castle," Ryland says as he looks down at the map.

"What are they like?" I ask. I have read many books on the royal family. I know there was once another family that ruled before the changed one destroyed everything. They died with the millions, and the royals we have now took the throne. I'm sure there's more, but I can't remember all the history I've read about them.

"The king is cruel, and the queen has lost her mind," he says, his voice dripping with hate. I don't understand his strong reaction, but to call the king cruel? *Cruel sounds like a personal word to use.*

"'Lost her mind'?" I ask, repeating his words instead of touching the subject of the king. I have heard little of his personality. My father always said he respected the king, but didn't respect the hunt on the changed ones. My father never told me anything important about the queen. Only once did he tell me something, and that was when he had a bit too much purple juice. The purple juice is what makes him fall over, and Everly told me they call it 'getting drunk'. My father said that the queen has beautiful, black hair before he passed out.

"There is so much you do not understand, Cassandra, and I wish you never learn any of it. It's best that you forget all of us when you step on to Fiaten and start your new life," he tells me. I can see he has shut down, and he won't look at me.

"I . . .," I say, but find I don't know what to say to him.

I have a feeling I couldn't forget these pirates if I tried.

15

RYLAND

"You feel drawn to her as well," Dante says as he comes in and shuts the door behind him. Cassandra has just left my room, and her entire body is drawing me in. *Everything about her is drawing me in.* I wonder if it's the same thing as my father felt for my mother. My mother is very beautiful, said to be even more so when she was younger.

"Perhaps," I say, not telling him anything. I have known Dante for years, since we were children, and when Hunter and I said we were leaving the castle, he came with us. I will always owe him for that. Dante has saved my life nearly as many times as I've saved his.

"We have both been around male changed ones

and seen how females are drawn to them," Dante says, not filling in the end of that sentence. The very reason we are travelling around is to look for male changed ones and take them back to Fiaten. The mountain is full of them, and they are being trained. The only problem is that Cassandra is a woman. I don't know how to explain to her that they are building an army in the mountains, an army to take back the throne. There are a lot of secrets on this ship, and I have no doubt she would run if we started to tell them to her.

"Cassandra is a very beautiful young woman, most men would be drawn to her," I say, moving to the table and looking over the map. The wind is good over the seas, and I know we will miss the guards' ship. The last thing we need is them finding us, or her. It would be one hell of a fight, and I won't give her up to the king. The guards would try to take me and Hunter to the king if they found us, but they would prefer to take Cassandra. I can imagine how happy a female changed one would make the king.

"She is indeed," Dante nods, as he rests back against the wall. I watch him closely, knowing my friend well enough. We don't let many women on board the ship, and we never sleep with the ones we take to different islands. If any of us need a release, we stop off at enough islands to find a woman to spend the night with. We just haven't recently, because the king is getting smarter, and we can't stay long on any island. So, having a very beautiful woman like Cassandra around is a distraction. *It's not just her beauty, it's her confidence and nature that are even more attractive.*

"No one is to date her, Dante," I say. If any of us were to get that close to her, it would only cause massive problems on the ship. I've noticed every single one of us staring at her.

"Why not?" Dante asks me with a smirk. There are so many reasons, one being the jealousy that it would cause. I saw the way we all looked at her, the way we all seem drawn to her. It's bad enough she has to sleep in one of our beds because the guests we have on board cannot be trusted with a changed one. They might try to kill her in her sleep.

"Dante, you can have any of the women, on any island. Stay away from Cassandra," I say, my tone sharp. *I wish Dante was frightened of me, but I know the bastard isn't.*

"No promises, Captain," he chuckles before walking out.

"Dante!" I shout after him as he walks out and

shuts the doors behind him. *By the seas, Cassandra is going to make life complicated for us all.*

The moment she crashed into our ship and crashed into our lives, Cassandra was destined to make things complicated for us.

16

CASSANDRA

"I was looking for you," Jacob says as he comes into the moonlight. It's the only light out here in the dark night. The wind howls through the night, and the sails catch the wind, making the night seem louder. I'm sitting on the steps on the deck of the ship after dinner, as I wanted to see the stars.

"I've been in the same place for over an hour, so you couldn't have looked well," I comment, and his lips turn up in a smile. Jacob takes off his hat and walks over to me. He sits on the edge of the steps like I am and leans back on his elbows.

"How was your first real day on the ship?" he asks me.

"Well, most of the people run away from me,

and the children look at me like I'm two steps away from eating them. I keep falling over when the ship rocks as I'm not used to the wet floors up here, and that cat does not like me," I say, and Jacob bursts into laughter, laughing so much that I end up joining in. It takes us a while to calm down.

"Salty Sam doesn't like anyone, so don't take that personally," he says. Well, I guess that's one thing. *My leg still stings from the scratches.*

"The cat scratched my leg as I walked past him earlier. I nearly jumped out of my skin," I say, and he chuckles a little as he bumps my shoulder with his.

"Have Chaz take a look at it, he will find some cream to help," Jacob says looking down at my legs, and then his eyes drift up my body until he gets to my eyes.

"I will," I say, leaning back and looking up at the stars to break some of the tension.

"Do you know the names of the ten stars?" Jacob asks me, pointing up at the nine stars that make a weird shaped circle. There is one star in the middle of the circle, but I don't know much about it. My father didn't know the names, and none of my books talked much of the stars.

"No, I don't," I reply.

"Well it's said that the star in the middle is called Love. That the nine stars around it were her lovers before they all died keeping her safe. They are called Fondness, Devotion, Adore, Lust, Desire, Warmth, Beloved, Sensation, and Compassion. Love couldn't survive without her lovers, so she died and joined them in the stars. The stars circle around Love to protect her, so she can be free to give her love to anyone who needs it. They say when you're alone, you only need to wish upon the star of Love, and she will help you."

"She had a lot of lovers then," I say, wondering how any woman could cope with nine men in her life.

"Some people are destined for more than one person," he tells me, and I look up at the circle of stars in the sky. I don't think on his words much more than I have to.

"Such a lovely story," I say.

"My mother told me it once and many other stories. She loved the stars," he tells me.

"So do I. As I grew up, the stars always seemed so . . . free. Something I thought I could never have, and I loved looking at them," I say, then think about a book I read. "I once read a story about the god of the sea."

"Would you tell me?" Jacob asks.

"The book said the Sea God lives in all the seas, and they say that the ones who truly believe can ask for a deal. Many ask for love, for fortune, and most for power. It said that the Sea God will make you a deal, but the deal always benefits him," I say, and he nods.

"Only the chosen will be treated fairly," he says. I look at him, and he shakes his head. "Something else my mother once said. She said her mother talked to the Sea God once. I do not believe it, but then again, there are stranger things in this world."

I silently agree with him.

"Would you tell me about your life?" he asks me gently.

"There is not much to tell. My father kept me hidden because of the mark, and I was found. So, I ran to the sea," I say. *I ran to sea and was saved by pirates.* Pirates who turned out to be better people than I could have ever expected them to be. How very odd, the way my life has turned out to be.

"I ran once from my past, and pirates also saved my life," he says and stops mid-sentence, changing his mind and standing up instead. Jacob offers his hand to me, and he pulls me up.

"Where are you from?" I ask as I stand up. Our

bodies are now pressed closely together, and he doesn't let go of my hand.

"I was born on Sevten," he tells me. We both just stare at each other, neither one of us looking away, and the urge to move closer to him is worse than before.

"You're sleeping in my room tonight, as I'm running the ship," he says, moving away slightly, but he keeps his hand in mine.

"I can sleep with the guests. I have no idea why you think I need to sleep in your rooms," I say, having to speak a little louder as the wind blows hard against the sails.

"Cassandra, remember how the people looked at you with fear?" he asks me.

"Yes," I respond, remembering the woman and how the other men have stayed far away from me today. I don't know how to explain that sometimes it bothers me how people treat me, how they fear me.

I'm not sure what to do as his fingers rub my hand, but it's comforting. I wonder if he knows how I'm feeling.

"People do unimaginable things out of fear. The very fact that they would hand over a baby to be killed, because of fear of what that child may or may not become, is proof of that. Let us keep you safe, because we do not fear you, Cassy," he says.

"Why don't you fear me?" I ask him, my breath haunting as he steps that little bit closer to me. Our breaths come out like clouds as the chilly night air blows around us.

"I do fear you, Cassy, but not for the reasons the others do. I fear you, because you could take my heart, and I would never want it back," he says softly. Jacob leans down, his lips briefly brushing mine before he sharply pulls away.

"Ouch!" Jacob shouts, stepping back quickly and rubbing the back of his head. I was so lost in Jacob's words and the ghost of a kiss, that I didn't notice Laura coming over to us. I didn't notice the fact that she just hit Jacob on the head with her wooden stick, and I try not to giggle. She lowers the stick and winks at me.

I have no idea why she just did that.

"Laura, how many times have we told you not to hit people with that damn stick?" Jacob says, still rubbing the back of his head.

"I have no idea what you are talking about," Laura says before walking off and whistling to herself. I watch her in disbelief and try not to chuckle.

"Don't laugh," Jacob groans as he takes my hand and walks us off, following Laura. I watch in surprise as she opens the doors that lead below deck and walks down them. The doors are about the size of her, and she is an old woman.

"She's stronger than she looks," Jacob says, making me giggle. "What did I say about laughing?" Jacob gives me a cheeky grin and picks me up, throwing me over his shoulder.

"Jacob," I say throughout laughs as he walks down the stairs with me. Jacob just tickles my stomach with his one hand, and I can't stop laughing.

"Should I ask why you have the little bird on your shoulder?" Hunter's deep voice comes from somewhere in front of us.

"She is being a pain in the ass," Jacob replies with a laugh and walks us past Hunter without waiting for his reply. I lift my head a little, just in time to see the smirk that Hunter gives me before he walks up the stairs. *He clearly agrees with Jacob.*

"Are you going to behave, Cassy?" Jacob asks before he slides me down his body. I'm way too aware of how every part of his body touches mine as he lowers me to my feet.

"Yes," I say, my voice breathless and strange to me.

"This is my room," Jacob says, leaning a hand past me and opening the door behind me.

"Thanks," I say, struggling to understand my feelings for the pirate. He nods, stepping back. I'm surprised he doesn't say anything about the near kiss, but I'm not sure if I want him to.

"Sleep well, Cassandra," he says before walking away. I watch him disappear into the shadows of the corridor before I walk into his bedroom. The room has a candle inside a glass lantern on the wall and one small window that lets in a little moonlight. There's a small bed with red sheets, and a large dresser in the corner. The dresser has a pile of books on it and a heavy-looking crossbow balanced against it. There is a holder full of arrows next to it. I look at the crossbow, knowing there's no way I would be able to even pick it up.

I kick my shoes off and take my coat off before leaving them on top of the dresser, loving the soft rug I can feel under my feet. The room smells like Jacob, and I'm concerned by how comforting that is to me.

"I'm going mad," I mutter to myself before walking over to the bed and realising that I need the toilet. I find his bathroom, which is similar to Chaz's, and quickly wash my face while I'm in there.

After I'm all sorted, I make my way back to the bedroom and slide into the extremely comfy sheets.

My eyes close in seconds, and my dreams are filled with handsome pirates.

17

DANTE

"You're not meant to be down here," I say before I lean back and throw a dagger into the wall opposite me. The storage room I'm in is at the bottom of the ship and full of boxes. They mainly have weapons in them, and cannons in case a ship targets us. That's very unlikely, and we haven't used them in a long time.

"I've never been down here, and I got curious," Cassandra replies behind me. I turn to see her standing close to the door to the storage rooms. She looks beautiful, as usual. Her dark brown hair is down today, the braids undone other than the one that holds the feather. I remember when I first saw her. She was standing watching the people at the party, not aware that every man's eyes were on her. I watched her dance with her friend. When her brown eyes met mine, I felt something; something more than just a base attraction. I felt drawn towards her. I was more surprised to learn that her personality is just as attractive as her looks.

"It's still not safe, pretty girl," I say and walk over to the wall. I pull out the four daggers in the bullseye painted on the wall of the ship. The walls are thick enough to do this down here and know there is no chance of making a hole. I place the daggers on top of a barrel next to me.

"Show me," she nods towards the wall. I simply smile slowly as I look over her body. The shirt she is wearing shows off way too much of her chest, and her breasts move up and down with each breath. The trousers are tied at her waist, showing her small waist and toned legs.

"Go and stand in front of the target, and I will show you," I challenge her. *She won't do this if she doesn't trust me.* I know I wouldn't hit her; I'm too good and have been doing this as far back as I remember. My father was a personal guard for the king, and my mother was a maid for the queen. I grew up bored in the castle, and my father gave me daggers to practice with. My father is known for being deadly with his aim and never missing, something I have inherited from him. Cassandra doesn't move, and I lock my eyes with hers. "Trust me?"

"Says a pirate," she says back, with a hint of humour in her eyes. I watch as some kind of decision crosses her eyes, and she moves towards the target. Cassandra stops next to the wall and pushes her back against it.

"Don't move," I say, picking up two daggers off the barrel.

"Don't hit me," she says.

"I would never hurt you, pretty girl," I say, flipping the dagger in my hand and throwing it. It lands right next to her arm, but doesn't touch her. I quickly throw the next one, and it lands next to her other arm, boxing her in.

"Impressive," she says, sounding breathless as I walk towards her. Cassandra isn't a short woman, but I am very tall, so I still have to look down when I stand in front of her. *She can't escape with the daggers caging her in, but she doesn't look like she wants to.*

"Can you fight?" I ask her, wondering if her parents taught her that.

"A little, but I only used to fight against my friend, who wasn't very good or interested in fighting. My teacher didn't know enough, and my father wouldn't spend much time bothering to teach me," she admits to me. I don't know why she seems to be embarrassed about that, but the slight blush on her cheeks as she looks down suggests she is.

"Your mother?" I ask carefully. I see a wave of pain cross over her eyes as she looks up.

"She died giving birth to me," she says eventually, after a long silence. I feel like she didn't want to tell me that.

"I'm sorry," I say, running my finger down her cheek, and she tenses up.

"All of you, you touch me like you personally care about me. You all have these nicknames for me and look after me. I don't get it. I don't get you," she says. I swallow the urge to ask about the others and how close she is to them.

"I do care about you, pretty girl," I say, and she watches me.

"Do you care about all the girls you bring on the ship?"

"No," I say, and the word hangs between us. I move away, pulling the daggers out of the wall and walk back to the barrels.

"If you ever want to practice fighting, I could

help you." I tell her, and she walks past me towards the door that leads to the stairs.

"I'll think about it, pirate," she says.

"And, I will think about you, changed one," I say, and she laughs as she walks out. I smile to myself, knowing that all I have done since meeting her, is think about Cassandra.

18

CASSANDRA

"So, this is Sevten?" I ask Ryland, who hovers next to me. I stand at the front of ship, watching the island coming into view. It's been a mad week on the ship, with me trying to get used to everything. Working in the kitchen with Zack is always the fun part of the day, while the un-fun part is trying to stay out of the way. The ship is chaos most of the day, but I like it. Most of my life has been quiet, and the ship is never quiet. Also, I'm rarely alone. I have slept in Chaz, Ryland, and Jacob's rooms all week. They said that next week will be Hunter, Zack, and Dante's turns to stay up at night. Ryland's room has the most comfortable bed, and I slept so well in it last night. I haven't seen much of the pirates, other than Zack in the kitchens and Chaz when he got me some cream for the scratches on my leg. He told me that Salty Sam does it all the time to everyone, and it's not worth getting infected.

"Yes, and where are you hiding?" he asks me, and I roll my eyes at him. Ryland has gone over the plan for me to hide in his room more than once. I suggested going below deck, but he said that's where anyone would look for someone. Ryland is worried someone might say something about me being on board, so he is leaving Dante to watch the ship. Dante is going to sit near the entrance to the ship and stop anyone from coming on board. It's a simple plan, and they are all clearly worried about me. Well, other than Hunter, who I'm sure would sell me off in a heartbeat for some gold or food. The evil looks he gives me make it clear he doesn't care much for me.

"In your room," I say, and he nods, looking back at the island with me. Sevten is about the same size as Onaya, but it's so different. The beaches are full of ports and different ships. The main city wall is visible as it's on the beach, and there are rows of green-leafed trees with brown fruits hanging off them. The city is built high, unlike our small houses, and they seem to have towers. The towers look to be made out of wood and are in block shapes. The city looks full of life and busy. I can't believe the amount of ships I can see from here. *There must be at least fifty of them docked.*

"It's so different," I say.

"And dangerous," he says, and I glance back as we get closer. I can now see that most of the ships have pirate banners. The place must be full of them, and what first seemed like a pretty sight is now a little frightening. I can't imagine all the different types of people that must be on this island. I see another ship, with big, dark green sails and a black-painted hull. It's so different from the others, and I know it's a guard ship. I remember my father telling me that the royal colour is a dark green, like the crowns the king and queen wear. The royal symbol is a green dragon on a black background. My father showed it to me once and said it was because the royal last name is Dragon.

"Time to go and hide," Ryland tells me, and I nod. I pass the seven people waiting to leave the ship, and every one of them watches me. The looks they are giving me are not pleasant. My eyes catch the beautiful woman who ran away from me, and she still looks terrified as she takes a step back. A warm hand grabs mine as I walk past, and I stop to look at Jacob who is standing with Chaz.

"Stay safe, we won't be long," Jacob says, and Chaz nods at me.

"I will," I say with a smile before walking away from them.

I don't say anything, just walk into Ryland's room. I close the door behind me and take a deep breath. I wander around his room, feeling the ship being stopped and hearing the shouts of my pirates. I stop with that thought. *Since when am I calling them mine?* They aren't mine, and I know that, but it's hard to think of walking away from any of them now. I walk over to the wall, which has five shelves; each has a bundle of things, including books. I pick up a book with a red spine and cover. There are no words on the outside, just a rose inside a crown on the cover. I sit on Ryland's bed as I open the book and read through it.

"The Dragon royal family were purely changed ones. Every single one of the royal line has been born changed, and they bring nature to life. I have witnessed the gifts, and they are truly wondrous. This was not a well-known fact but those of us who are close to them, know it. The royals do not appear in public. We know how the queen has no power without her king, and the king is the changed one. It draws

people to him, like it did her to him many years past. It seems to only work when they are near each other. The changed king could have any wife, but the princess Lauraina was the one he chose.

The newly born daughter with pitch-black hair, has the mark and is a changed one. There have been no female changed ones recorded for many years, so to have a royal female is a wonder.

The child is sweet, and her parents care dearly for her, but they argue. There have been harsh disagreements between them, and it's well-known that the king is having an affair with a maid. It is not well-known that there was a fair-headed child born. A child who was not changed and taken away by the mother. The queen would have left the king if she found out. They both have lovers, but bastard children are another matter. I wonder what that child will be like when she is older.

I wonder what the changed royal will be like when she grows up and takes the throne.

I flip over to the next page and start reading more.

The child has grown into a beautiful woman, with long, black hair and dark blue eyes. The princess has found four chosen men and they have been named the four princes of Cal—"

"In here," a male voice says, stopping me from

reading the rest of the book, and I look up as the doors to the room are opened. Two dirt-covered men walk in, and I slide the book onto the bed as I stand up. They both have deeply tanned skin that is covered in dirt, rag-like clothing, and when one of them grins, I can see a mouth full of cracked teeth. Being honest with myself, this is what I thought pirates should look like when I imagined them. *I wonder where Dante is.*

I can't see him just letting them come in here for me.

"The girl was right, a changed one. I'm glad we paid her well," one of the men says in a crackly voice. I can just about make out what he's saying. The accent is so different, deeper than I'm used to hearing. The pirates' accents are like mine, so there is little difference.

"She will fetch a few pennies and ten barrels of food," the other man replies, and I laugh.

"You have to catch me first, boys," I say, and they both grin at me. I ignore the fear I feel as they step forward, moving around the big table. I glance quickly around the room and mentally cringe when I see there are no weapons. *Damn it.* The big sword is gone. I bet Ryland took it with him. I should have thought to have a weapon in case this happened.

"Maybe we should have some fun with her first?" the one man asks as he looks me up and down. I've always liked the way the pirates look at me, but the way he does, makes me want to be sick. I would rather die than let them touch me. The fear I felt before is worse now as I back away and towards the window. The glass looks thick, and I know there isn't anything heavy enough for me to throw through it. I still glance around desperately.

"No, she is worth too much money, and she is a changed one. They will pay more for her to be untouched," the other man says, and I don't pause in my search, but keep my eyes on them. They move closer with every step, and my heartbeat is too loud in my ears for me to think straight.

"Shame," the other man draws the word out slowly as they get closer. I pick up the heavy paperweight off the table. At least it's something.

The men nod at each other, splitting up and going to either side of the table. I'm trapped unless I can knock one of them out. Choosing to wait is a bad idea, so I do the only thing I can think of. I jump on the table and run across it, jumping off the other end and running towards the door. I struggle to pull it open, and when I do, I run straight into something hard. I bounce to the floor and look up to see another man, holding a sword at his side. The man is just as dirty as the other two and has a crooked smile. My mark starts burning for the first time in my life. I have never felt anything from it, but I have to put my hand on my head, and then I see a little brown hair behind the man's feet. I move slightly to the right of the man and see Dante on the floor, blood pouring from a cut on his head. Someone has tied his hands and feet up, too. My mark just burns more, and everything is going blurry.

"Be a good girl now," the man says, and he points the sword down at me. The tip touching the end of my chin, he moves it slightly, and I wince at the pain as he cuts me. I know it's only a little cut, but it hurts all the same as he presses the sword closer to my neck. The mark is burning more, and all I can think about is getting to Dante. *I need to know he is okay.*

"Come on, the auctions start soon, and we need to get her there," one of the men says behind me, and a cloth is held over my mouth.

My last thought as I scream and kick at my kidnappers is, *I hope Dante is alive*, just before everything goes black.

19

CASSANDRA

"Wake up, changed one," a female voice says, shaking my arm. I groan, wiping my eyes with my hands, which feel dusty, and blinking my eyes open. I look up to see large metal bars in a dimly-lit room. Looking around, I see I'm inside a large cage, with bars all around. The ground is dusty, and there's a young girl sitting in front of me.

"Who are you?" I ask as everything comes back to me. The ship and the men who took me. I glance down at my clothes, seeing them all in place, and nothing hurts. I only feel sick and a little dizzy as I watch the girl. She has long, curly, brown hair, and she looks to be in her early teens. The girl is too young for the serious expression she has.

"Do you have any powers that could get us out of here?" she asks. Her voice is panicked, and I look away from her to see where we are. The room is empty, other than the two of us and one door with a little light coming through it. The walls are high, and there are two big gaps in the ceiling which shine light through them. The walls look like they are made of a cream stone, and the floor is nearly all sand.

"No, that's just a rumour. The mark is nothing," I say, and she laughs as she pulls her hair out of her face. The girl is very pretty, but I don't understand why she is here with me. *I don't even understand what I'm doing here.*

"Where are we?" I ask her.

"In one of the storage room for the auctions," she says plainly. I should have guessed those guys kidnapped me to sell me. I reach up and touch my mark, feeling that it's still warm. I remember Dante on the floor, and sickness crawls up my throat. *He has to be okay*. The other pirates will come back, and Chaz will help him.

"Why are you here?" I ask her to distract myself from thoughts of Dante. I can't help him, and sitting here worrying isn't going to get me out of this mess.

"My father sold me to the auctioneers," she says and looks away from me. The girl has a ragged dress on a thin frame and cuts on her arms that I can see. Her accent is like Dante's, but a slight bit different. She has strange shoes on that wind around the lower parts of her bottom legs.

"What's your name?" I ask her, and she looks up at me. Her sea-blue eyes are bright, and she has a round face. I like that she isn't scared of me, but then again, it could be that she has little to be scared of anymore. *We are going to be sold at an auction soon.*

"Olivia, but my friends call me Livvy. What's yours?" she asks me.

"Cassandra, and we need to get out of here," I say, and she laughs. The laugh is sad, and when I stand up, she goes quiet. I watch as she pulls her knees to her chest and wraps her arms around them.

I walk around the cage, pulling at the metal bars and finding them all firm. Shaking them does little difference. I find the door, pulling on it, but it has a big padlock on the outside. It's impossible to open. I shake on it again and again until I kick it in frustration. *Stupid door.*

"Unless you have powers that can blow this cage

up or dig us a hole out of here, we can't get out," she says, and I look down at her. I know she is right. I imagine that if I did get us out of the cage, guards would still be waiting right outside those doors would be guards waiting. There is no way they would leave me unwatched.

"If I had those powers, we would be leaving," I say with a deep sigh. Neither of us say anything as I walk around the cage, pushing against the bars again. I can only hope the pirates notice I'm missing and find me. *I think they would come after me, but who knows?*

I don't know why they would, when they don't owe me anything. I owe those pirates my life, and if they save me, I would owe it to them twice over. *I wonder if they will just leave me here to my fate.*

"Why did your father sell you?" I ask the girl. She looks up at me, resting her head on her knees.

"For money and food. The people here will do anything for it, and I'm a pretty girl, unlike so many here. One of the pirates who run the auctions, saw me one day. The next day, I was thrown into a cage. My father didn't look my way as they took me, and my mother screamed. My little sister—" she stops, her voice catching for the first time. I don't move as she wipes her eyes.

"My little sister was ill and needs medicine and some food to get better. In the end, my father didn't have much choice, and my life was always going to end in the auctions. I know I will be dead or wishing I am soon. The only thing I can be happy about is that my little sister will survive," she tells me. *So much responsibility for someone so young.* I guess it must be easier to accept, if you knew this is where you would always end up. I just can't imagine how strong she must be to do this. To not run.

"I'm sorry," I tell her, and she just looks at the ground.

"There were girls I grew up with, sold much younger than I am. I believe I'm lucky in a way, so do not be sorry for me, Cassandra. I feel sorry for you," she says. Her words make me look at her in confusion. I'm sure we will both have the same fate, but mine will be a quick death at the hands of the king's guards. At least, that's what I hope for. I don't want to be taken to the king.

"Why?" I ask quietly, knowing I don't want to know the answer.

"They will breed you like a horse," she says, and her words fill me with disgust.

"Why would they do that?" I ask, and she finally looks up at me. Her eyes are full of tears.

"To have changed children and sell them. Every child you have would keep them rich," she says. "There is no way you will be given the gift of death for many years, and if you ever get a chance to kill yourself, do it. Many, many do before they get to the auctions, and I wish I had." Her words are haunting and make me slide to the floor. I have always expected death, not anything else. *I would rather kill myself than be a puppet for some man.* I would never let anyone take a child from me, just to sell them to the king.

"Why is it this way? All for a stupid mark," I say, my words echo around the room.

"Because the Sea God kisses his special children on the forehead. Leaving a mark. The Sea God chooses them and gives them untold power," she says.

"What does that mean?" I ask. I have never heard that before. I don't know much about the changed ones and the Sea God. *I wonder how linked they are?*

The doors open before she can respond, the light flooding the room and making me squint my eyes. I stand up, and so does Livvy. When I can see more of the room, there are two men walking towards the cage. I watch as one of them unlocks the door. They both walk into the cage, swords at their sides and sinister grins on their faces.

"Come," the man says grabbing my arm, and I don't fight him. It's pointless for me to try while he holds a sword that could end my life in seconds. I wonder for a second why we aren't in handcuffs and my eyes drift to the sword. I know that they don't need to cuff us, because they could just knock us out or worse.

The other man grabs Livvy and drags her out of the room. Her vacant eyes meet mine. She has given up all together. The light is brighter outside, and I use my arm to cover my eyes. When I can see, there are hundreds of eyes on me. We are being pulled through a crowd and people are whispering and pointing. The people look well-off, with shiny, multicoloured clothes and big figures like my father. When we break out of the crowd, I see the big wooden stage in the middle. There are three women on the stage, and people are shouting prices in the crowd. I pull my eyes away and look up, seeing only tall, wooden, house-like structures that tower into the skies. People are hanging out of the windows, looking down and cheering. The strange thing is, there is so much colour and yet not one tree in sight. There isn't any wildlife or plants around, either, just sand paths and tall, wooden-built houses. They make it seem like it's night, as they block out the sun.

I hear 'changed one' shouted louder and louder throughout the crowd.

"All sold," the man in the middle of the stage says, clapping his hands as we get closer. He has long, black hair in dozens of tight braids that match his dark skin. The man is dressed in all black, with gold bands around his wrists. There are at least three on each arm, and they seem to almost glow. I can't pull my gaze away from them and I almost trip on a rock, but the man holding my arm roughly pulls me up.

"I have a special treat for sale today! Not only do we have a very beautiful, untouched girl brought up on Sevten, but we have a female changed one!" The man shouts the end part, and the crowd cheers. They start clapping and cheering so loudly I can't hear anything but them as I'm dragged up the stairs of the stage. The man holding me, chucks me into the man on the stage. He holds me at a distance, his hand tight on my arms as I try to move. It doesn't work as he pulls me to his chest and holds a hand across my chest, while his other arm is wrapped around my waist.

"She is a pretty one as well!" the man shouts, and the cheering gets quicker as I try to get out of his clasp. I don't like him calling me pretty or how he's holding me close. His foul-smelling breath is unavoidable as he moves his face close to mine. I wriggle against him and smile when my hand wraps around the dagger in his belt.

"So, how much would you give me for a female changed one? She would be perfect for breeding with a gorgeous body like hers. Just imagine all the changed children you could have and the money from them!" The man shouts, and a wave of disgust fills me as people start cheering. I glance around, seeing the men's stares and the small bags of gold they are pulling out of their pockets to pay for me. I won't be paid for, and I'm not letting this man sell me. I look up at the man, and his greedy eyes watch the crowd. He's not watching me at all, like he should be. I wait until people start shouting numbers out before bending my spare hand behind me, reaching for the dagger in his belt. He doesn't notice as I slide it out of the holder. With the dagger firmly in my hand, I do something I know will get me killed. I slam it into his stomach, the dagger sliding through easily as it's so sharp.

The man looks down at me in shock before his

eyes glass over, and he stumbles away from me, his hand going to the dagger in his stomach. I walk slowly over to him, standing close as his mouth gapes open.

"I will not be sold to anyone, and may the Sea God take you to hell, where you belong." My words are loud, and the crowd is silent, hearing every single one of my words. I don't take them back, and I watch as he falls to the ground. I back away from the middle of the stage as the two guys who brought us out pull out their swords. The man holding Livvy throws her onto the ground and her eyes look at me with panic. I turn to run when an arm wraps around my waist. I go to push the person away when I look up to see Hunter smiling down at me.

"Such a naughty little bird." He laughs as he pulls his sword out and pushes me behind his back. I watch as Hunter blocks a blow from one of the men, moving quickly to slam a kick into his stomach and pushing the sword through the man's chest as he straightens. Hunter pulls his sword out as the other man comes over. They fight for a long time, their swords clanging against each other, and it's clear this man is a better fighter than his dead friend. My heart is in my chest as Hunter is caught on the arm by the other man's sword, and I see it bleeding. My mark starts burning as I watch the blood drop down his arm, but Hunter doesn't waste a second as he hits back, managing to catch the other man off guard and slamming his sword through his chest, through the man's heart. Hunter leaves the sword in the man's chest, and picks up the dead man's sword, holding it at his side as he walks over to me. Another man gets on the stage, his hands in the air as he watches us. This man has long, black hair, light gold skin, and is not far from our age.

"We will be leaving now. Don't follow," Hunter says to him. I watch as he takes a small bag out of his pocket and throws it on stage. The bag opens as it lands and gold coins roll all over the stage. *How in the seas did he get all that money?*

I know that amount is a fortune, enough to buy half an island. The man nods, running towards the bag and picking up the gold. *Clearly, it's enough to buy me.*

"Come on," Hunter says, turning to face me and wrapping an arm around my shoulders. The moment he touches me, I feel safer than I have in hours, and I look up at the pirate. He saved me. I was saved by these pirates more times than I want to admit. I wonder where the others are. I can't say I expected Hunter to come after me or to be holding me close like he is.

"No, we have to get the girl I was with," I say, stopping him by putting my hand on his chest. I look up into his dark blue eyes that match every part of his dark personality. *Dark, but beautiful.*

My hand feels warm as my fingers graze the skin on his chest where his shirt dips open. I don't know why I did it, but his deep breath makes me look up at him again.

"Cassandra," he says, and I can't miss the warning in his tone, but I don't want to listen to it. The sounds of people shouting and everything else dies away as we stare at each other. We could have been anywhere in the world, for the way he looks at me is something I would have trouble ever forgetting. My gaze skims over his face, seeing the little dents here and there from fighting, the little stubble he always has that looks soft, and finally, the soft lips that are open slightly.

"Coming up next is a stunning young woman. I hear she has never been touched, and look at all this soft, brown hair," a male voice says, snapping me out of my thoughts of Hunter and those damn lips.

"Hunter, please. I can't leave without her.

Please, for me," I plead with him. I don't know what crosses over his eyes, but I don't move as I mentally beg him to save Livvy for me. I know begging him anymore wouldn't help, but I can't leave her here. *I can't save everyone, but I won't lose her.*

When he gives me a simple nod, I suck in a deep breath. Hunter is going to do this for me. The pirate that I never thought even liked me, has saved my life, battled two men for me, and now is going to save someone else just because I asked him to. He reaches into his jacket and pulls out another bag around the same size as the last one. Hunter pulls me with him back to the steps of the stage and walks up them.

"I want the girl as well," Hunter says and throws the bag of gold towards the man who is on the floor picking up the gold from the last bag.

"Deal," the other man on the stage says, the one holding Livvy tightly in his grip. Her tear-filled eyes meet mine, and she sags in relief against him. The man lets her go, and she runs into my arms.

"Thank you. I will never, ever forget this," she says to me, and I don't reply. I didn't save her, Hunter did. I will have to thank him. I still don't know why he changed his mind.

I hug her tightly, and then she holds my hand as

I let her go. I urge her with my eyes to stand tall and not let these evil people see her fear. *They don't care.* Hunter grabs my other hand as we walk down the stairs, and he starts leading us out of the crowd. I keep my eyes on Hunter's back, not looking at the people around me who whisper and watch us as they move out of the way. I glance down at my hand, seeing the blood on my fingers and try to block out the sight of the man's shocked face as he died. *I killed someone.*

I took his life, and my last words to him were something I read in a book about the Sea God. How the damned are dragged to hell by him.

We come out of the crowd and through a tunnel that leads to a long path full of little carts. I can't stop looking around as Hunter drags me through the crowd. There are so many different types of people, all with their eyes watching me in shock. The wooden houses look bigger this close, with wire hanging between them and clothes being dried in the wind. There's smoke coming out of many of the rooms, and the place is just so noisy. There is so much going on that I don't know where to look. A woman with light-pink hair walks past us, her dark eyes catching mine in the crowd, and she smiles gently. I smile back, surprised when she stops walking and bows low to me. A few people walk past, and when I look back, the woman is gone. *Why would she bow to me?*

Hunter walks us faster through the crowd, not slowing once in his large strides, and he shoves some people out of the way. A massive group of people stop in front of us, causing us to stop in the middle of the path as we wait for them to pass us by. This part seems like a shopping district, full of little carts. The carts seem to be selling a range of different things, from clothes to food. There is one with different-coloured eggs that catches my attention. There are five large eggs, all different colours and held in glass cases.

"Hunter, what are those?" I ask him, pointing in the direction of the table. Hunter looks over at them and then back at me with a little laugh.

"Dragon eggs," he says. My eyes widen as I look back at the table. I heard there were dragons in the mountains, but, apparently, they are extremely rare. I don't want to know how hard it must have been for the man to get the five eggs on his carts. I wonder if they are real at all. I don't have much more time to think of it as Hunter starts moving us down the path again, and I have to concentrate on not falling over as we walk fast.

"Where are the others, and is Dante okay?" I ask him, raising my voice a little over the noise of the people we are passing to get to the sea. I can see the ships and the port now in the distance.

"They are checking all the auctions. We weren't sure which one you had been taken to, and Dante is fine," Hunter explains as he walks us down the long pier and towards the ship. I can see our ship right at the end, with Chaz standing near the plank of wood that leads up to it. When he sees me, he smiles and nods. His eyes drift to Livvy before giving Hunter a strange look. I imagine he's wondering why Hunter brought back more than one girl. I look up in time to see Hunter shake his head and give me an annoyed look. I resist the urge to smile at him.

When we stop in front of Chaz, he moves closer to me and lifts my chin. His finger gently moves across the little cut there, and his eyes narrow.

"You okay?" he asks me gently as he lets my chin go. I nod, feeling in a little bit of a daze as I think about his caring nature. I wonder if he is this lovely to everyone, and if it's only me who feels bothered by it. *I like it too much, the feeling of being cared for.*

"Pretty girl," Dante says, coming down the

wooden plank from the ship. I let go of Livvy and run into his opens arms. Dante holds me close, and I take a deep breath,

"You're really okay. I saw you on the floor and—" I say, looking up at him. I gently trace my finger across the cut on his forehead.

"The bastards caught me off guard, but I'm sorry for letting them take you. I won't ever let that happen again," he says, making my breath catch.

"Dante—" I start to say, but Hunter cuts me off.

"I will find the others," Hunter says before walking past us. I watch him go, and he looks back when he gets on the ship. Our eyes meet, and he smirks before he walks away.

"Come and see me later," Dante says and lets me go. Livvy runs to me and takes my hand.

"Why don't you take your new friend on board and clean up in my room?" Chaz says, his voice soft as Livvy bursts into tears.

"Shh," I say, holding her to my side. Unsure what else to do, I give Chaz a panicked look. He simply nods his head towards the boat with a smile. I don't know what to do with her, but I guess taking her on the ship is the next thing to do. *What am I going to do with Livvy when I get off the ship at Fiaten?* I guess she could come with me, but I don't want to put her in any danger.

I take Livvy on to the ship and to Chaz's room, not seeing anyone else on the way, but I do look. I want to see them all, make sure they are okay and back on the ship. *What is wrong with me?* Once we are there, she sits on the bed with me and just cries softly until she falls asleep. My hand goes to my mark, remembering the burning feeling. I have no idea why it did that, and I remember the book I was reading.

What is a changed one's chosen?

I try to think of anything else as I don't have any answers. I'll go and find that book again; it seemed to have a lot of useful information, but I have no idea what queen they are talking about. I try to keep my mind on the book and off of what could have happened today and what *did* happen. *I killed someone.*

The sight of his cold, lifeless eyes fills my mind, and I get off the bed, leaving the room and walking down the corridor. I find my way to the dining room and sit in a chair, just staring at the wooden table. I don't know how long I sit quietly, only moving my gaze when the chair next to me is pulled out. I look up to see Zack as he sits in the chair next to me and places his glove-covered hand over mine. I've never seen him without those leather gloves on, and I wonder why he doesn't take them off. I try to focus on the feeling of his hand over mine; the warmness of it and knowing Zack is with me.

"Hunter told me you killed the man who was selling you," he says. His tone is gentle and holds no accusation. I look up into his eyes and nod.

"That man would have killed and sold thousands. You may have killed him, Cassandra, but his soul was already tied to death. He deserved death, and the Sea God would only thank you," he says and stands up. I almost miss his hand when he moves away and walks out of the room.

Is my soul marked with death now? Or has it always been for the mark I was born with?

20

CASSANDRA

"Thank you, Cassandra," Livvy says before she walks down the stairs to the lower decks and the bed the guys have said she can stay in. They offered her a similar deal to me, a safe trip with food and a bed. She just cried when Ryland told her this, and I patted her back. I wasn't sure what else to do. Livvy explained how she can't believe she has a chance to live and finally off Sevten. I think it's just a lot of pressure for a girl her age to handle. I know I'm only three years older than her, but my life has made me strong. Hers has, too, and I hope that reflects on her future. I hope I'm around to see her find some kind of happiness.

We left Sevten a few hours ago with ten new

people on board, and they all wish to travel to Fiaten, like me.

"Collecting strays, are you?" the crackly voice comes from behind me, and I turn to see Laura stood there. Laura has on a strange, white dress, with circles all over it, and a yellow ribbon holding her hair back. A matching yellow ribbon is tied around the walking stick she's leaning against.

"Not exactly," I say. I wouldn't call Livvy a stray, more an adopted member of the ship. *Like me.*

"My grandson likes you," Laura says.

"I didn't realise you were related to anyone on this ship," I reply.

"Hunter and Ryland are my grandsons. When their mad father went too far, they took me with them on this ship. They feared their father would kill me. They were right, he would have. He had already taken my only daughter from me, and those children suffer enough for that. It turned Hunter cold and Ryland strict," she says, her blue eyes watching me closely. She doesn't look a bit like Hunter, but her eyes are like Ryland's. *I should have seen it before.*

"Is she dead?" I ask.

"No, but there are far worse things than death. Sometimes, someone can love a person too much to let them go, and my daughter paid a price for that kind of love," she says, and I wonder what price was paid. It doesn't make much sense.

"I'm sorry, Laura," I say.

"Perhaps you need to read more of that book in Ryland's room. It may answer more questions." She smiles softly.

"How did you know I read that?" I ask, and she laughs.

"I told you this was my ship, girl," she says.

"That you did." I smile, and she taps me on the arm with her stick.

"Dinner is ready, changed one," she says, walking away from me, and I follow her. I hate when anyone calls me 'changed one,' but the way she said it, was like it's a gift. The useless mark seems to define me, and I would never call it a gift. *It has given me nothing.*

I walk into the dining room following Laura, and I'm surprised to see all the guys sitting around the table. When I glance at them all, I see that Hunter is missing. Laura takes the seat in the middle of Ryland and Chaz. Dante stands up and holds a seat out between his and Zack's. I sit down, and he pushes me in before taking his own seat. Jacob is sitting opposite me, and he smiles widely when he sees me, his eyes tracing over every part of my face. I pick up my drink to break the silence that has filled the room; every single one of the pirates are looking at me. *I can feel it without looking.*

"A present," Hunter says from behind me, making me jump and cough out the water I was drinking. My eyes widen when he puts a large, dragon egg on the table in front of me. The egg is about the size of my head, the shell is a shiny sea-blue, and there are tiny white dots all over it.

A dragon egg from the market on Sevten. The island we have just left.

"Hunter, by the seas," Dante says, his voice dripping with shock. Just like how I feel. Hunter has brought me a dragon. *An actual dragon.*

"Why did you buy her a dragon?" Ryland shouts, and the room goes silent. I place my hand on the egg. It moves slightly and feels warm to the touch.

"The little bird wanted it, and now she might actually be able to fly," Hunter says with a laugh as he sits down and gives me a smirk. Whatever his excuses may be, I still think there is another reason for him buying me this dragon egg. Hunter doesn't seem the type to buy something just because someone wanted it. I watch him closely as the others talk.

"We are on a wooden ship, in the middle of the sea, and you thought buying her a dragon was a smart idea?" Chaz says.

"It's not a fire dragon," Hunter explains as he scoops potatoes off a tray in the middle of the table and onto his plate.

"You have never bought anything for a woman before, and the first time you do, it's a dragon," Laura says and starts laughing. Hunter looks at me briefly and sharply turns away. I don't understand him, but the gesture is making me want to understand him more.

"Ice, it's an ice dragon, and a big one, apparently," Hunter finally says as all the guys glare at him.

"Thank you, Hunter," I say softly, and he grins at me.

"I hope it eats you, would save us all the trouble," he says, and I laugh, Chaz and Zack joining in. I really hope he's joking, and that the dragon isn't going to eat me. Or even worse, freeze my hand off when it's born. Zack picks the egg up as he stands and puts it on the spare seat next to him.

"Any dragon egg care advice?" I ask them all, my eyes still drifting to the egg.

"I had a dragon once," Laura answers me as I put some chicken meat on my plate. Zack slides an apple over to me, and Dante puts potatoes on my plate too. It's strange how they always do this, they always put more food on my plate. I like how Zack always remembers to put an apple on my plate, because he knows they remind me of my home.

"Calaria was an earth dragon, not as rare as that one you have, but she was a gift to me. They need only a little care, they look after themselves and those they believe are family to them. When they are hatched, they only need meat to survive. I have heard ice dragons are found in the water a lot, so perhaps this dragon will be good at hunting fish," she says.

"How big do they get?" I ask because my books never spoke of their size. I knew dragons existed, because my father told me so. He said there were far more before the land was destroyed and they died. I also know the royals all have dragons. Fire dragons. The king is said to have the biggest one in the world. I have never seen the dragon he has, as he never brings it along when he travels around the islands.

"As big as a very large horse. Some people used to ride them back in my day. They live for fifty years, but my Calaria was killed," Laura says and eats her food.

"How did–" I start to ask, but Ryland interrupts me.

"How long until it hatches?" he asks, changing the subject, and I see him give a strange look to Laura. She seems to understand as she nods.

"Did your books teach you nothing other than dragons exist? All those books you were forced to read as a child, when all you wanted was to be fighting." Laura laughs, her voice crackly.

"I know this, they take around eighteen months to hatch," Chaz says.

"Did you ask how long the egg has left?" I ask Hunter, who shakes his head.

"No," he says and goes back to his food. That doesn't surprise me, so it's going to be a guessing game for when this egg hatches. *It could be any day.*

"You're staying in my room tonight. Come on, you should have an early night as you had a long day," Dante says next to me, and I nod at him. Zack hands me the egg after I stand up, and it's very heavy. I resist the urge to drop with the egg to the floor and instead, hold it close to me. I expected it to be cold, but it's not; it's warm. I guess even ice dragons are warm.

"I can stay and help you clean up," I offer, and he smiles.

"No. Like Dante said, it's been a long day for you," he says, and his fingers skim over my hand on the egg.

"I'm glad you're safe, I should have told you that before, my little fighter," he says and steps back. I nod, feeling his words connect with me, and I move away, clearing my throat. When I turn, I catch Laura's eyes as she watches me. Her look is a simple smile, but her eyes seem like they are figuring something out about me. I wish I could figure something out about her.

"Good night," I say to them all after I pull my eyes away from Laura. They all say goodnight as I walk out the door, following Dante. We go to his room, both of us quiet as we walk. Dante holds the door open as I walk in and he lights a candle in a lantern for me. Dante's room is smaller than the rest, with just a bed and no window. There is a painting on the wall of the sea. *Strange to have a painting of the sea when you're on a ship.* The room is warm and cosy, making me want to get into the bed as I suddenly feel tired. It's been such a long day, and I just want to forget most of it. I don't want to forget the way Hunter looked at me or the feelings I seem to be having for Dante. Well, the feelings I have for all of them. How can I like them this much in such a short time? I couldn't face losing Dante today, and I've only known him a short while. What will my feelings be like for him and the other pirates when we finally get to Fiaten?

How long will it be before I fall in love with these pirates, as they slowly take my heart with each day?

When Dante shuts the door, he snaps me out of my thoughts. I place the egg on the small chair in the corner of the room and pick up a blanket off the small dresser. I wrap the egg up, just in case. I also pick a spare pillow off the bed as Dante watches and put it on the floor in front of the chair. Just in case the ship moves. When I turn around, Dante is lying on the bed and looks comfy.

"Come here, pretty girl," he says, patting the bed next to him as he lies on his side. My cheeks go bright red as my mouth parts. Dante looks so attractive tonight, not that he hasn't always been. His shirt is laced at the top, but left open, so I can see the muscles of his chest. His hair is cut short and he has a slight beard, which suits him. I glance at his muscular arms and down his body.

"I can't lie in bed with you, Dante," I say with a chuckle.

"Please? I thought we lost you today, and I just want to hold you. Nothing more. I just need to feel you close to me," he asks me, shocking me enough with his kind words that I find my feet taking me to him. I slide off my flat shoes before getting on the bed with him, and his arm snakes around my waist, pulling me against his hard body. I don't feel myself breathe as I tuck my head under his chin and place my hand on his chest. We stay like this for a long time before Dante speaks.

"When the others came back to the ship and woke me up, and you were gone—" Dante clears his throat and then continues speaking, "all of us panicked. Until that point, I didn't realise how much I would miss you. I know it's a lot to ask, but could you stay on the ship with us and not leave?" Dante asks. Each word feels like an arrow to the chest.

"Dante," I say gently as his hand slides down my face, then lifts my head up, and our lips meet. He moves his lips slowly against mine, giving me time to respond, and I gently move my lips like he does. Dante controls the kiss, but he is gentle, each kiss sweet and slow. I can't think straight until he breaks away and looks at me.

"I can't make you stay with us, and living with

pirates isn't safe, but think about it." Dante says and gently kisses me again before letting me go. I sit up as he rolls off the other side of the bed and walks to the door,

"Goodnight, pretty girl," Dante says before he opens the door.

"Wait, Dante. Are mermaids real?" I ask him, and he laughs.

"One kiss doesn't get you that answer," he says, and I glare at him. I pick a pillow up and throw it at him. He catches it and throws it back at me.

"Dante," I say using a more serious tone, and he smiles.

"Mermaids are real," he says and turns to walk out. *I knew it*. I wonder what they look like, what they are like.

I place my fingers against my lips, still able to taste Dante's kisses. My first kiss was with a pirate, and I'm surprised that I don't regret a second of it.

21

CASSANDRA

"So, how are you settling in?" I ask Livvy as we clean up the dishes in the kitchen after breakfast the next morning. I can't stop smiling, and I know it's because of Dante's sweet kisses. He only smiled at me this morning over breakfast, but everything has been a little mad. There are four new men on the ship, all extremely thin, and they ate a lot at breakfast. They have been offered the same deal as Livvy. I'm starting to realise that the pirates take on homeless and desperate people. They offer them food and safety as they travel around. There is also a family of four: two children and their parents. They are mainly cleaning the ship, and I've seen the black-haired children running around the ship.

It's really rather sweet. Yes, sweet how they help these people who need it. If only people on Onaya knew what the pirates were really like. I have no doubt that most pirates are not like these, but still, they should be recognised for the good things they do.

It's not what I expected from pirates, but then again, these pirates are nothing like I would have expected at all.

"Fine. I have my own little room down there, and it has a lock on the door, so no one can get in. Everyone is nice, but—" she stops mid-sentence.

"But?" I ask as she hands me a plate to dry with the dishcloth.

"I always expected to die on Sevten, and now, now I have life ahead of me. I have no idea what to do or how to be happy about it," she says, stopping the washing up and moving away. I put down the plate and lean against the counter.

"My life changed a lot in one day, and I found that it's best to just take it one day at a time. Life can throw a lot of arrows at you, and yes, one may hit you, but most will miss, and you will forget about them. This is just a part of your life, and one arrow won't stop you," I tell her, and she smiles at me.

"You're right," she says.

"Do you have any hobbies? Anything you really wanted to do if you could," I ask her.

"I know it's nothing special, but–" she starts, then seems to change her mind.

"Tell me," I say, bumping her shoulder, and she laughs.

"I just want to find a good man, settle down, and have some children. I want a simple life where I know my family will be safe," she says.

"That is a special plan, and I want you to have it," I tell her.

"And, it's an unrealistic plan," she says.

"No, it's not. I want the same things, too, you know. I want a family and a life. I want happiness and a world where I don't have to hide," I say.

"I want that for you, too, and who knows? Maybe we will have that," she says. *I hope we do, too*. We clean all the dishes up, and I walk out of the room to find Chaz leaning against the wall. Chaz's blond hair looks like he's run his fingers through it several times, and his jaw is freshly shaven. He looks really good, and I take a step closer to him without thinking about it. *These pirates draw me in too much.*

"I wanted to talk you, if you have a second?" Chaz asks, and I nod.

"I'm going to go and have a look around,"

Livvy says and hugs me before she walks off. I'm not used to her being so friendly, but I guess she has become a friend to me because of what we went through together.

"So, is everything okay?" I ask, and he nods. Chaz holds out a hand, and I slip mine into his as he walks us down the corridor and into his room. The room is lit up from the bright sun shining through the window. It's still a little cold down here, and I shut the door behind us.

"I bought you some new clothes when we were in Sevten," he says, offering me a big bundle of blue and black clothing.

"You didn't have to. These must have cost a fortune that I can't repay you," I say, holding the soft clothing closer.

"We are pirates, and we have a lot of gold," he winks, and I laugh. It doesn't surprise me they have gold as they couldn't afford the amount of food they have on board otherwise. They also couldn't afford to help as many people as they do. I wonder where they got it from in the first place. I place the clothes on the bed and have a look through them. There are three blue tops, and black, tight-looking trousers. There are also two blue dresses that look normal to what I used to wear back home. There are also three pairs of thick socks.

"Oh, and these," he holds up a pair of long boots. They look like they would go up to my knees, and he puts them on his bed. I run my fingers over the thick leather.

"Thank you," I say and walk over to him. I don't know what inspires me, but I throw my arms around his neck and hold him close. He doesn't move for a while, but when I try to move away, his arms go around me, holding me close.

"Every time you're near me, all I want is to be closer, Cassandra," Chaz whispers, his mouth near my ear, and I freeze.

"I–" I manage to get out, and he kisses my ear gently, making me freeze again. Chaz feels so warm this close to me, and I have the urge to bury my face into his chest. I know I'm attracted to him, how could I not be, but I kissed Dante last night. I may not have much experience with people or relationships, but I know about jealousy. I got jealous every time I saw the love between Everly and her mother, Miss Drone. That kind of jealousy is cruel and threatens to take you over.

"You shouldn't want to be close to me. I mean, I

knocked you out with a book," I say, trying to make the situation funny and stop my heart from pounding.

Chaz gently kisses my ear again and whispers, "Oh, Cassandra, you would have to do far more than hit me on the head with a book to stop me from wanting you." He chuckles lightly, then lets me go, and I step back. I don't say a word, and neither does he, but his eyes show humour. I turn around and go back towards my clothes on the bed.

"Cassandra, I did get you something else," he says, and I turn my head to give him a quizzical look. *What else could he think of getting me?*

"I'll have to repay you somehow," I say, and he shakes his head.

"No need," he says and pulls out a necklace from his pocket. The necklace is a triangle with a bright-green stone in the middle. The shape of the necklace is similar to my mark, but it's beautiful and made out of gold. I have never been given a gift like this before, and all the jewellery I had was lost to the sea. Even then, it was never given to me. My father just didn't say anything when I found it and started wearing my mother's necklace. Mind you, he wouldn't speak much of her at all to me. I wish I knew more about her sometimes, and now I know it's too late to find out anything more.

"Can I?" he asks, holding up the necklace, and I nod, speechless.

"Thank you, it is so pretty. I've never been given anything like this before," I say as I hold my hair up, and he puts the necklace on. Chaz's fingers skim my neck and send shivers through me before he steps away.

"Beautiful, stunning, and unique. Those are words I would use, but they are also words I would use to describe you," he says, and I let my hair fall down before I turn to him. I can't process his sweet words, knowing they are ones I won't forget.

"Why do you wear this necklace?" I ask him, stepping closer and skimming my fingers around the different shells.

"There is one from every island, all seven. I collected them to remind me of something,"

"Of what?" I ask.

"That all of us are connected, even if the islands aren't joined together anymore. I believe we can one day have peace, and I will fight my whole life to see that day," he says.

"There will never be peace as long as the king

hunts the changed ones. When he hunts me," I say, looking down and letting my hand fall.

"The king won't live forever," Chaz says, and I watch as he moves to sit in the chair in the room.

"What do you read in here?" I ask him, following him over.

"Mainly books on healing, but this one is on dragons. I was looking for anything useful about your egg," he says, reminding me of my dragon egg in Dante's room. I'll take it with me to whoever's room I'm staying in tonight.

"Did you find anything?" I ask, and he shakes his head.

"No, but there is one more book to read." He points at the blue book on the table. I pick it up and go to sit on his bed. I miss reading. It's been too long since I sat down with a new book. I read all the ones in my house, and eventually, I just re-read everything.

"What are you doing?" he asks me as I get comfy and open the first page. I know it's strange, but I missed this so much.

"Reading. We can look together, and I like to read," I tell him, and he smiles widely.

"Me too," he replies and looks down at his book. My eyes trace his large body and his slightly messy hair that looks like he has run his fingers through it one too many times.

Chaz is really handsome, but I force myself to look down at the book.

These pirates are way too distracting.

22

CASSANDRA

I look up at the water as it falls from the shower, splashing all over me, and think about the new feelings I'm having for all these pirates. I mean, they are pirates, and I'm in here wishing Everly was here, so I could ask her questions about men.

Questions about what I'm feeling for them all and how I'm drawn to each of them.

I turn off the shower and dry myself off with one of Chaz's towels. I pull the new, tight, black trousers on, and they stick to my legs and stop around my waist. I tuck the simple, blue shirt into them, then pull my thick socks on and love how they feel. Then I pull on the knee-high leather boots that I'm surprised are my size. *Did he measure my feet when I was out cold?* I pull my hair up in a band, leaving the braids out to shape my face. I don't know why, but I find myself wanting to look nice for these pirates.

I look over at myself in the small mirror inside Chaz's bathroom. My brown eyes are bright today, and I feel strangely content with everything in my life. I'm on a pirate ship, and I'm, I'm happy.

"They look . . . you look–" Chaz mumbles out when I come out of the bathroom. I know I'm not sleeping in his room tonight, and we have spent the whole day reading in here. Chaz explained earlier that he isn't one of them that are running the ship tonight. We found a lot of information about dragons in the books. Like how they need warmth when they first hatch and how they grow to five times the size of when they are born in a couple of weeks. Unfortunately, there weren't any drawings in the books of ice dragons. We found interesting drawings of some fire dragons, but Chaz thinks they will be very different.

"Thank you," I say, and he nods. Chaz's door is opened, and Zack walks in, stopping in his tracks as he looks me over.

"You look older, more . . . *beautiful*," Zack says. The word 'beautiful' is said slowly, like he doesn't want to say it. Zack looks over at Chaz as he stands and moves next to me, his arm brushing against mine.

"Cassandra, you're staying in my room tonight," Zack says, and I nod. I started to realise that there is no point trying to argue with them about staying in their rooms. *It's not like I'm sharing a bed with them, not exactly.*

"Okay, thanks. I need to get my egg from Dante's room," I say, and he nods, offering me a glove-covered hand. I let my hand brush Chaz's fingers as I walk past him and towards Zack, sliding my hand into his as we walk out.

"I already got it and placed it in a box with a blanket in my room," he says, and I smile widely up at him.

"Thank you," I say, and he nods, rubbing the back of his neck and looking away.

"Night, Cass," Chaz says behind me, and I turn to nod at him, my eyes wandering over him before I let Zack pull me into the corridor.

"I made you some food, since you missed dinner," he says as we walk down the corridor. His blond hair is wavy today, looking soft and newly washed. Zack smells like cooked food, but then I wouldn't expect much less from someone who spends most of the day in the kitchen. *It's comforting.*

He leads me down the corridor and opens the door nearest the kitchens. The room is larger than I expected, with a long, flat bed on one wall and two small windows. There is a desk in the one corner with a lantern on it, flooding the room in a soft-yellow light. There is also a guitar resting against the bed, sheets of paper on the bed next to it. I go over to it, running my fingers across the wire strings.

"I have only seen guitars in books. I've never heard one played before," I say to myself more than Zack, but he hears me anyway.

"Can I play for you?" he asks me. I turn my head slightly and catch his eyes.

"You don't have to," I say.

"I want to," he chuckles, moving over to me. I sit on the bed, picking up the plate of food and start eating. Zack chooses to sit on the chair by the desk. He places the guitar on the floor between his legs as he pulls his gloves off. I can't see them too much in the dim light but what I can see makes me stand up and walk over, leaving my food on the bed.

"What happened?" I ask as I pick his hand up in my own. I know it's rude to ask, and we don't know each other well, but I feel like I want to know. *I feel like I want to know everything about these pirates.*

"I told you once that I paid a price for killing my parents, and the price wasn't just what is on my back," he says softly as I run my fingers over the dozens of little white scars all over his hands.

"This is why you wear gloves all the time," I say in a whisper.

"They are not a nice sight, neither are the lashes I received on my back," Zack tells me, and I let go of his hands to tuck his hair behind his ears as it falls around his face. He catches my hand with his and holds it over his face as his head rises to watch me.

"You didn't deserve what they did to you," I say softly, and he moves his head slightly to the side to press a kiss into the middle of my hand.

"Cassandra, you should be careful with your words. Men will fall in love with you for your sweet words," he says and lets my hand go.

"They are not sweet, just true," I tell him, brushing my fingers across his hand once more, and he looks down at his hand.

"My little fighter. You are going to fight a way into my heart, and I hope I get yours in return," he says with a crooked smile as he looks up at me. I don't reply, feeling my cheeks blushing, and the room feels like it's getting warmer.

"Go and sit," he says softly and with a small smile on his face.

I sit on the bed and start eating my food again as Zack picks up the guitar and starts playing. The tune is slow, each note feeling like it's drawing me into the song more. Zack hums along with the song, his eyes watching the strings as his fingers move effortlessly across the strings.

Zack plays like someone who was born to; every note is perfect and makes me want to cry with how deep the song is. I wonder if it hurts his hands to use them like that. From the scars, I believe they must have broken more than once and cut many, many times. My mark starts burning a little as I stare at his hands.

When Zack stops playing, his eyes meet mine, and my lips part open. I miss the sound of his song and the soft hum of his voice.

"What did you think?" he asks, his tone gruffer than I'm used to hearing from him.

"It was flawless," I whisper, and I don't just mean the song.

23

HUNTER

I watch Cassandra from a distance, her hair whipping around her shoulders from the cold wind and her arms wrapped around her chest as she watches the sun set over the sea. *The view is stunning, and I wish I meant the sun setting.* The yellow and orange light shines over her face, highlighting her high cheek bones and the softness of her skin. Cassandra's hazel eyes reflect the orange tones of the sun as it disappears, looking like it's sinking into the ocean. I've seen dozens of beautiful women in my life, but none draw me to them like she does.

"Little bird," I say, moving to stand close to her. I want to be close to her, a feeling I'm not used to having. I have a suspicion of why that is, but I'm not foolish enough to test it. I glance at her mark and force my eyes away. Going anywhere near that mark would be beyond foolish.

"Hunter," she replies, her eyes looking up at me, and a little smile appearing.

"Dinner is ready," I say, and she nods, pulling her eyes away from me and walking towards one of the doors of the deck. The men we have on board are scrubbing the deck and she moves effortlessly around them, each one of them looking at her. In fear or desire, I'm not sure. She seems to get both reactions from most people.

My mother was, and is, the same.

"You're staying in my room tonight. Don't touch anything," I say to her when I pull the door shut and walk down the stairs. She's waiting at the bottom and gives me a slightly evil grin,

"I will touch everything then," she says, and I grab her arm, pulling her small body against mine.

"Are you teasing me, little bird?" I ask her.

"Always, pirate," she says back, making my gaze draw to her sweet lips. Just as I'm about to kiss her, something hard hits me on the back of my head. I let go of Cassandra and turn to see Laura standing there.

"I told you once before that I'm taking the stick

off you and throwing it in the sea if you hit me again, grandmother," I say, and she smiles up at me with an innocent grin.

"I am the boss of this ship and I will hit you again, boy." She holds the stick up in the air. I swear by the seas, I want to kill this old lady. If she wasn't related to me, I swear to the Sea God I would have left her on an island somewhere.

"You are not the boss," I grit out.

"I am," she puts her hands on her hips, the stick hitting my leg as it's at a weird angle. I move backwards and look up at the ceiling.

"I just can't deal with this madness," I say and storm out of the corridor, hearing Cassandra's laugh behind me and hating that she makes me smile.

What is it with this girl?

A girl I can't stop thinking about, and she is slowly driving me insane.

24

ZACK

"Find anything useful?" I ask Chaz. I glance at the massive pile of new books he bought on Sevten a week ago. Every book is about changed ones, the ones who used to be worshipped. People don't know what it used to be like for the changed ones, and the only reason we do, is because of the people in the mountains on Fiaten. They protect the changed ones. The only problem now, is that I don't want to send Cassandra to Fiaten. *I don't want her to leave.* I look down at my hands, remembering how she looked at me. It wasn't with disgust like I expected. No, it was filled with lust. *Possibly with love.* Something I never thought I'd be lucky enough to have.

"Nothing about a female changed one," Chaz

says, sitting back in his chair and pushing the book shut.

"The king will be sending every guard to find her after the auctions. There is no way someone didn't recognise Hunter," I say, keeping my tone neutral, but Chaz still picks up on something in my tone as he looks over at me. It's hard to keep how worried I am out of my tone. I would kill anyone who tried to take her from us, and the only one that would stand a chance is the king.

"She's lovely. The books never say anything about the beauty of a changed one. The only other female changed one I've seen is very lovely, too," he says, and I nod, looking away. We all know how that ended for everyone. Hunter and Ryland know best.

"She is beautiful," I say.

"She understands so little of men and doesn't realise how she is with us all. I don't want to confuse her, but I have feelings for her. I won't lie to you or anyone else about that," Chaz says, and I nod. That's true. She would have picked up on all our feelings for her by now if she knew what she was doing. It doesn't surprise me that he has feelings for her, I know all the guys do. When we realised she was missing, we *all* went mad. I should have known one of the guests would mention the changed one on our ship. We paid them not to mention her, but that clearly didn't work. I believe fear seems to dictate people's minds when it comes to changed ones. They don't listen to logic, because they fear the powers of the changed ones. People don't understand how the powers work. Changed ones need their chosen before they can use their powers. Cassandra doesn't have any chosen or we would have known. *Chosen are always protective or in love with their changed one.* I think back to when we had a changed man on board. I don't know how he was hidden, but we found him running away on Foten. He had three women with him, all wearing his mark on their foreheads, and they all loved him dearly. He explained that when he marked them as his chosen, he then got a gift with the first. The second and third enhanced his powers.

"I want her to stay on the ship," I tell Chaz, and he doesn't seem shocked.

"Me as well, but we can't all have her," he says seriously, leaning back in his chair.

"Why not?" I ask, and Chaz laughs.

"We would end up killing each other," he says. I think about seeing him with Cassandra, and my hands tighten. I don't know how I would feel, but I couldn't let her go now. Cassandra will always need the protection of all of us, unless we let her go. Fiaten would be the only place that could keep her safe, but I can't do it. I can't let her go, and I know I would follow her anywhere.

"I would never harm any of you. You saved my life more than once, but I feel something for her," I tell him.

"Let's just see if she wants to stay first. I don't believe she will," Chaz says and looks down at the floor.

"Then I'm going to give her a reason to stay," I say. Knowing at this point, there isn't any other option. *This ship is my home, and I want it to be hers, too.*

"So am I," Chaz says, making me laugh before I walk out of his room.

So that makes two of us. Two out of six.

25

JACOB

"What are you doing, Cassy?" I whisper, and she jumps. I laugh quietly as she looks around at me and puts a finger to her lips. I nod and move next to her as she hides behind the barrels in the room. I came down to get some spare blankets we have down here and found her hiding. She points to the hole between the barrels, and I look through just as I hear voices.

"Ha, I win," Roger says, sitting and playing chess with Livvy. I watch as Livvy blushes and tucks a bit of her hair behind her ear.

"Can we play again? And maybe you could teach me that move?" Livvy asks.

"I'd love to show you, Olivia," Roger says, and

then he clears his throat. I lean back, and Cassy takes my hand, leading us up the stairs and into the corridor before she speaks.

"They are so sweet, don't you think?" she says with a cheeky grin. Cassandra looks lovely today, more relaxed and happy than I've ever seen her. Truly stunning. Her hair is down, longer than it's ever been, because she has taken all the braids out except the one with the brown feather. I glance at her tight clothes, long boots, and the shiny, green necklace that stands out on her chest.

"They have become close, but I guess that's because they're similar in age," I say, and she nods.

"Do you know why Roger is a permanent member of this ship?" I ask her, and she shakes her head. I take her hand in mine and lead her down the ship, pushing the door to my bedroom open. I sit down on the bed, and she sits next to me. I like how relaxed she is around me now, around us all.

"We found Roger in the middle of the Lost Sea. His family had lived on a tiny island there for years, maybe as long back as when everything was destroyed," I tell her. I remember the journey well, we were looking for something, but never found it. A crown said to have power enough to destroy the king. Instead, we only found shipwrecks and dangerous waters. We will have to go back, but we need to find out more information about the lost crown before we do that. The Lost Sea is full of mermaids; they have their own city under the water. They wouldn't let us near the sunken ship we needed, the one said to have the crown.

"How did they survive?" she asks.

"They had coconut trees and built some kind of tunnel to get fresh water. Honestly, they were lucky until the mermaids found them," I say.

"Mermaids?" she asks with wonder.

"I haven't seen one, but Roger has. They killed all of his family and he escaped in a boat. When we found him, he was close to death," I say, remembering the stick-thin shell of a boy we found.

"So, why does he stay on board?" she asks me.

"He says he wants to learn to fight like us and avenge his family by killing the mermaids that killed them. I don't blame him, but he is foolish to think he has a chance against them. So, we keep him close and make sure he doesn't do anything foolish on his own." I tell her.

"What do you do for fun, Jacob?" she asks me, lying back on the bed. I watch her quietly before pulling the box out from under my bed. I lay it on the bed and open it as she sits up.

"What are those?" she asks, looking at the three long crystals in the box. They glow blue and sometimes move, but that's only when we get close to the mermaids.

"They're called mermaid hearts," I tell her, and she looks at me strangely before looking back at the crystals. She goes to touch one, and I grab her hand.

"You can't touch them. Not you," I say, looking at her mark, and she nods.

"These can heal people and are said to be made by the Sea God for the mermaids. I don't know if that's true, but I had four of them, and when Roger was dying, I pressed it against his heart and he lived. The crystal disappeared the moment it touched him," I tell her.

"That's amazing," she says, and I shut the box. I slide it under the bed and look at her.

"I collect rare things. I have others I could show you if you want?" I ask her. She nods and gives me a small smile. We spend the rest of the night looking at the things I've collected, and she doesn't seem to get bored of me. When I fall asleep later that night, I know I found the rarest thing in the world when I jumped into that ocean after her.

26

CASSANDRA

"Does it move much?" Livvy asks as she sits next to me, looking down at the dragon egg in my arms. I lean back against the cold wood of the ship, feeling the cold wind whipping my hair to the side. The last two weeks on the ship have been normal, well, as normal as they can be. The pirates have been busy planning and running the ship. I've seen them the most when I've been sleeping in each of their beds. When I stayed in Ryland's room, I looked for that book I read and couldn't find it. I asked Ryland, and he wasn't sure what book I was speaking of. I'll have to find a moment alone with Laura to ask where it is. *I have a feeling she has it.* The old woman seems to disappear in the day when I go to look for her. The weather is a lot colder today, and the water is harsher and rocking the ship more. Every time I breathe, a cloud appears from the cold. Thankfully, it isn't raining, but the dark skies suggest it's not far away. I look to the left, where I can see the distant island of Foten. It's nerve-racking being this close to the king. *The man that's hunting me.* The pirates never speak of the king, and anytime I bring up the clear fact that he will be after us, they tell me not to worry. Livvy clears her throat, reminding me that I've not replied in a while.

"Sometimes, but come here and put your hand on the egg," I say, and she does.

"Can you feel the heartbeat?" I ask, and she nods, a big smile spreading across her face. I run my hand over the top of the egg. The heartbeat is a new thing that's happened in the last few days. *I wonder how long we have left before the egg hatches.*

"I'm going to stay out here a little longer. Would you take the egg inside?" I ask her. She smiles widely and picks the egg up off my lap. It's getting heavier with each day, and I see her struggle to hold it. I laugh when she quickly walks off with it. I'm guessing it's so she can put it down quickly. I stand up, smoothing down my dress and pulling Dante's coat around me tighter. I walk over to the wheel, seeing that it's locked in place by some rope. I haven't seen it closely before, and I can see the silver handles now. They look like solid silver, and I wonder how expensive that was to have done.

"Do you want to steer?" Ryland asks as he comes up the steps, his eyes watching my hand on the wheel. I don't know why, but I almost feel guilty for touching it.

"Yes," I say, knowing that it would be a strange but brilliant thing to do. Ryland comes over and unhooks the rope holding the wheel in place. He waves a hand towards the wheel in front of him, and I walk over. I place my hands over two handles, and Ryland moves behind me, his hands covering mine, and his large body pressing mine against the wheel. The wheel is lighter in pressure than I would have expected it to be. The cold wind whips my hair into my face, and I try to blow it out of the way.

"Just gently move the wheel, we still need to stay straight," he says, his words making my cheeks feel warm as he steps closer to me. Ryland's whole body is pressed against mine, feeling so warm, and I rest my head back without thinking about it.

"Sure," I say and tilt the wheel until Ryland

stops me. The ship moves slightly to the left, and I move it back again.

"Those clouds don't look nice," I comment, pointing to the left. The ship isn't aimed in that direction, but they look black.

"That's the Storm Sea. No ship survives the journey other than the guards', and we don't go that way. We go around the top of the island of Fiaten and dock on the other side, in the Cold Sea," he tells me. *I guess that makes sense.* I don't know much about the Storm Sea, but my books suggested it's impossible to cross. The Storm Sea is in the middle of Foten and Fiaten. In one of my books, there's a drawing of the king's castle. It's on the edge of a cliff overlooking the Storm Sea, and the sea was drawn with whirlwinds and massive tornados. I wonder if his castle is actually like that. *I hope I never find out.* It's the last place I would ever want to be.

"Isn't the Cold Sea full of icebergs?" I ask after a while. Ryland's hand lets go of the wheel and slides down my side. He leaves his warm hand on my waist.

"Yes, but they are easier to avoid than a tornado and whirlpools," he says, a smile in his words that I don't need to look at him to see. I look back at the dark skies, lightning flashing through them. The sea is so dark, too, like it's angry with the world.

"What is that?" I ask, pointing to the dark shadow moving through the water, coming straight out of the Storm Sea. Ryland looks over and gently pushes me out of the way, spinning the wheel sharply to the left, in the opposite direction to the ship.

"The guards' ship! Get the cannons ready!" Ryland shouts down the ship, and his voice echoes as fear fills me. I look down just in time to see Hunter nod at us before shouting his own demands. I look back to see the other ship is sharply turning towards us; the dark green sails can now be seen. The ship is all black, with large, silver cannons on its sides. At the front is a silver dragon statue that almost looks like it's cutting through the water. Its massive mouth is wide open.

"Go and hide, Cassandra. It's you they want, and we are not letting them take you," he says, and my eyes narrow on his.

"Where?" I ask him, just as he straightens the ship out and rain starts pouring from the skies. The speed of our ship is not good compared to the speed of the guards' ship, which is catching up. I stand watching him, my clothes being soaked by the heavy rain, but nothing matters other than the way he looks at me.

"My room. Now, go!" he commands me, and I force myself to turn and walk away from him. I gasp when he grabs my arm before I can leave. Ryland gently pulls me to him and kisses me.

A deep, demanding kiss that shocks me as much as it sends warmth throughout my body. The kiss is brief, but powerful, making me want to never stop kissing him. Ryland lets me go and his hand goes behind my head, pulling our foreheads together.

"Cassandra," he says as our foreheads meet, and a bright green light appears before my eyes. I feel a warmth from my mark that fills me slowly, and I can hear nothing. I can only see the bright green light until it disappears, and everything comes back in a rush: the loud sound of the ship cutting through the sea, the sails being pushed by the wind, and the cold rain as it pours down on us. When I can open my eyes, Ryland is still close to me, and he pulls away slightly with a parted mouth. Ryland stands staring at me, his eyes wide in wonder, and then I see it.

A mark is on the middle of his forehead, just like mine. The same place, the same black colour, and I stumble back. *What the hell was that?* I try to think if anyone has ever touched my mark before, and I can't remember. *I don't think anyone ever has.*

"I knew it," Ryland says with a big smile as he tries to reach for me, but I move backwards, holding up my hands. I don't understand why he is happy about this. I've just given him a life of being hunted by the king, and the guards are on their way to us now.

"I'm sorry, I didn't–" I get out as I take big steps backwards.

"Cassandra, it's not–" he starts to say when something loud bangs into the side of the ship, and I lose my footing. I slide across the wet floor, and my back smacks into the wooden wall. My whole side hurts, but I pull myself to my feet, seeing that the guard ship is right next to ours. I lean up over the wooden side of the ship, and I can see they have landed a big plank of wood between our boats. The guards are rushing on to the ship.

"Here, take this, and then we need to talk when we get out of this," Ryland says after he runs over to me and hands me a small dagger. The dagger is bright green with a black handle.

"Stay behind me," he says, pulling out a large sword from behind the wheel. The sword is silver, and it glows a faint green when Ryland lifts it up.

The guards run up the steps, and Ryland meets them before they can even step on to the bridge. His sword meets theirs, and he kills the first man without even trying. I pull my gaze away from the fighting just in time to see a guard picking Livvy up and dragging her by her hair across the deck as she holds on to my egg for dear life. I can see Hunter holding a big sword and he swings it down over the head of a guard running on to the ship. I look away to see Dante on the side of the ship, daggers in his hands, and he is throwing them at the guards on the plank. They fall into the ocean as he hits them. The ship rattles again when a cannon fires loud and hits the lower part of the ship. Livvy's scream shakes me from just looking, and I know I have to help her. My pirates all have their hands full and can't help her. Her screams are begging me to help as she looks up at me. I flash a look over at Ryland, surprised to see him handling his own with at least ten guards circling him.

I climb over the wooden wall and jump down onto the main part of the ship, running with my dagger in my hand over to the guard who is dragging Livvy towards the plank of wood.

An arm wraps around my waist suddenly, the force knocking me off my feet, and I fall to the ground, the dagger slipping out of my hand and sliding across the ship.

"No!" I shout, feeling my mark going warm, and I struggle against the guard.

"Time to go," a man says from behind me, and I turn my head to see a middle-aged guard looking down at me. The guard is dressed in all dark green, with a sinister grin, and he picks me up like I weigh nothing. I kick at him and struggle to get out his grip as he throws me over his shoulder and walks over to the edge of the ship. I scream, feeling my hands burning and look down to see my hands dripping with water. *What in the seas?* I struggle more, kicking and screaming for him to let me go. The guard picks me up by the back of my coat and holds me in front of him. My feet are hovering above the ground, and water is falling from my fingers, mixing with the pouring rain. My eyes catch Hunter's on the other end of the ship over the guard's shoulder, seconds before something hard is smacked into my head.

There's a look of fury in his eyes, a look of promise, and a look that tells me all I need to know.

My pirates will save me.

EPILOGUE

HUNTER

"I'm going to kill every one of those guards. I knew a few of them that escaped," I spit out as I watch the ship sail off into the Storm Sea. We can't follow them there, and they know it. Our ship isn't designed for those waters, and my father would use his powers to destroy our ship when we got close. His castle overlooks those seas.

Bastards.

"They won't kill her. They're taking her to the king," Chaz says, wiping one of his daggers free of the blood on it. Every one of the guards who walked on to this ship are dead, and I glance over to see Jacob as he throws the bodies into the sea. That girl Cassandra brought aboard the ship is missing, too, along with the dragon egg.

The ship is wrecked. The cannons did a good job of making sure we can't follow them for a few days while we repair it. Jacob and Zack fired as many cannons back as we received, but had to stop when they got Cassandra on their ship. They moved the plank too quickly for us to stop them. All I saw was the guard throw her over his shoulder and then whack her on the head with the back of a dagger. I ran for her, but I was too late. They had her.

I remember how I grabbed a rope and tried to jump over to the other ship, but they had a good head start by then, and I couldn't make it. *I had to watch them take her.*

Ryland comes down the steps and I see him for the first time. My hands tighten when I see Cassandra's mark standing out on his forehead. The upside-down triangle. Each changed one has a different mark.

"You're one of her chosen?" I ask, not wanting to believe it.

"Yes," Ryland says. Cassandra will have her power now, even if it's weak. The more people she chooses, the more power she gets. My mother had four, and was powerful. My father found a way to take her power, all of it. Now, the shell of the woman who was my mother is all that is left, and her other chosen are dead. *Killed by my father.*

"We have to get her back before he gets her," I say, and no other words are needed.

"Time for us to go home, brother," Ryland says. Home to a place where I swore I would never return to until I could kill my father. A place full of horrors and memories I don't want to remember.

But, Cassandra is there, my little bird.

"Time for us to see our father and get our girl," I say as I see Jacob coming over to us. He looks as furious as we all feel. I glance over at each one of my friends, seeing their nods and knowing the same thing as we do.

Cassandra belongs to us, and no one is taking her.

Saved by Pirates series continues with *Love the Sea*...

AUTHOR'S NOTE

Hello and thank you for buying my book! You're amazing, and I can't tell you how much I appreciate your support. A big thank you to Michelle, Taylor, Anna, Meagan and Chesca.
A review would be amazing, and I would love you for it.
Thank you to all my family for their support.
Please keep reading for the first two chapters of Winter's War, Her Guardians series book four…
(Out December 2017)

ALSO BY G. BAILEY

The King Brothers Series-

Izzy's Beginning (Book one)
Sebastian's Chance (Book two)
Elliot's Secret (Book three)
Harley's Fall (Book Four)
Luke's Revenge (Coming soon)

Her Guardians Series-

Winter's Guardian (Book one)
Winter's Kiss (Book two)
Winter's Promise (Book three)
Winter's War (Book Four)

Her Fate Series-

(Her Guardians Series spinoff)

Adelaide's Fate (Coming soon)
Adelaide's Trust (Coming soon)
Adelaide's Storm (Coming soon)

Saved by Pirates Series-

Escape the sea (Book One)

Love the sea (Book Two)

Save the sea (Coming soon)

One Night series-

Strip for me (Book one)

Live for Me (Coming soon)

The Marked Series (Co-written with Cece Rose)-

Marked by Power (Book one)

Marked by Pain (Book two)

Snow and Seduction anthology-

Triple Kisses

The Forest Pack series-

Run Little Wolf- (Book One)

Run Little Bear- (Coming soon)

Protected by Dragons series (Five book series)-

Wings of Ice- (Book One)

Wings of Fire (Coming soon)

Wings of Fate (Coming soon)

LINKS

Here are all my links,

(I love to be stalked so if you have some free time...)-

♥Join my FB Group?♥-

https://www.facebook.com/groups/BaileysPack/

♥ Like my FB Page?♥-

https://www.facebook.com/gbaileyauthor/

♥Be my FB friend?♥-

https://www.facebook.com/AuthorG.Bailey

♥Add me on Twitter?♥-

https:twitter.com/gbaileyauthor

🖤Check out my website?🖤-
www.gbaileyauthor.com

🤍Follow me on Amazon?🤍-
http://amzn.to/2oV9PF5

🖤Sign up for my Newsletter?🖤-
https://landing.mailerlite.com/webforms/landing/a1f2v0

27

ATTICUS

Wake her up, wake her up, new King. For the crown will fall, the crown will fall.

The shaking of the ground wakes me up from my deep sleep and strange dream. I can't remember anything other than words about waking someone up, and the childlike voice that sung them. I glance over at Winter, who is pressed to my side, her arms wrapped around a pillow. The room is still dark, the stars lighting up the sky outside, and it's cold. Colder than I remember it being. Winter moves slightly, rolling onto her stomach, and her hair spreads across the pillow.

My mate.

I smile when I see the marks on her back, a

beautiful reminder of last night. The phoenix, wolf, tree, and wings. I've waited so long to be mated to her, to my Winter. We finally have everything, and even with her grandfather causing issues, I know we will make it through this.

The room shakes again, and this time I know it's not a dream that woke me up. I sit up and pull myself out of bed, careful not to wake Winter up. The room shakes again as I throw on some jeans and a shirt.

What the fuck is going on?

I storm out of the bedroom, and there's a dark witch outside. Some older woman that I don't know, but she bows to me.

"Watch Winter, and do not let anyone in this room. If she wakes up, tell her to stay inside," I say, and she straightens up.

"Yes, your highness," she says, and I pull on my power to lead me to the throne room. The room is in chaos when I appear in the middle of it. Demons are attacking, and there are at least fifty in the room. One runs straight to me, with a large, silver sword. I quickly pull on my fire power and throw a line of fire towards him. The demon possessed man doesn't even move out of the way as the flames head towards him and burn him into nothing.

There was no scream, and that's the weird part. It's like he didn't feel anything. How can you fight against demons that don't care if you hurt them?

"They want the queen," a witch runs over to me. I cover her when two demons follow her by using my wind power to throw them out through the glass windows.

"How do you know that?" I ask, lowering my hands.

"The king let Taliana's parents out from the dungeons. I was there, and the demon king said he wants Winter," the woman pleads, she looks familiar, but I don't know her. She clearly cares about Winter, and that's enough for me to believe her. I pull on my power to try and find her, it doesn't work. I can't feel her, only darkness. *No.*

I use my power to take me to my bedroom and find our bed empty. I pull the door open, and the witch is gone. The castle shakes again, and I use my power to find to Jaxson. There isn't a witch strong enough to move the ground like this, and the whole castle is shaking. I appear in the gardens, the trees are on fire, and a dead witch looks up at the skies from my feet. I stand straighter when two demons run at me, their grey skin and the empty look in their eyes giving them away. They have big, silver swords raised at their sides and use wind to divert the fire in the trees towards them. They don't stop walking as the fire engulfs them, and they burn, the awful smell filling the night. I lean down and close the witch's eyes, she is so young. A growl gets my attention, and I look to my right, seeing Jaxson.

Jaxson has split a hole down the middle of the royal gardens, and he is in wolf form and is ripping the heads off demons as he runs past. He is massive like this, taller than a human, and it's easy for him. The witches are using their power to push the demons into the hole. Some are using wind and most are using fire, I'm proud of how they are working together. Light and dark united. I try to find Winter again, finding I can't; there's nothing, but I'm not giving up. *I will find her.*

"*Jaxson!*" I roar into his mind, when a demon runs at him from behind with a large, silver sword aimed at his head. I pull my power and lift the demon off the ground, throwing him into the hole.

"*Winter is gone!*"

I shout into his mind, even over the witches' screams, the distance between us, and the noise of the shaking ground.

Jaxson's threatening growl is the loudest, most dangerous sound.

28

JAXSON

I pull my wolf back and shift, pulling the jeans off the floor where the demon I just killed had died. Atti's words repeating over and over in my mind. She can't be gone, not now. A demon runs at me, but Atti runs over, pulling a sword off the ground and swings it across the demon's head.

"Where is she?" I growl out when Atti gets to me.

"I can't find her, I can't sense her, D," he says, his words filling me with panic. She can't be dead, I would know. Our mate isn't dead.

A demon runs at us, and Atti shoots a fireball at him, burning a hole in his chest, and he collapses into blue dust. I stomp over to a demon, who is holding a young witch on the ground. She is struggling to hold him off with her air power.

"The whole city is under attack. Atti, you're their king, and you need to tell them to go the castle!" I shout as I pull the demon off the witch on the ground, throwing him into the hole.

Atti closes his eyes, his body glowing a yellow colour as he tells the whole city to leave,

"Everyone leave and go to the goddess' castle. It's safe, and I'm showing you the image now. Everyone go, leave the city, and you will be safe,"

I hear the same thing as the witches do, and they start disappearing. Atti stumbles a little, his hands going to his knees as he takes a deep breath. *That must have been a fucking lot of power.* I grab Atti's arm, shaking him a little, and he nods at me. This isn't the time. We need to find Winter, and we can't do that here. He straightens up and flashes us back to the goddess' castle, straight to Wyatt and Dabriel, who are pacing Winter's bedroom.

"Winter feels gone, where is she?" Wyatt shouts walking over to us, and Dabriel follows. They both look as panicked as we feel.

"I can't feel her," Dabriel says, and I nod. I feel empty, like the place inside me where she was, is empty now. I can't sense her, like I've always been able to since I met her.

Fucking hell she'd best be alive, or I'm going to destroy the world until I find her or kill myself. There isn't a life without Winter. I can't lose her, not now.

"Wait, I feel her," Atti says and grabs our arms.

I feel a flicker of something, just before Atti takes us to Winter. To our mate.

WINTER'S WAR

Her Guardians series-
Winter's Guardian Link
Winter's Kiss Link
Winter's Promise Link
Winter's War Link

EXCERPT FROM IZZY'S BEGINNING

Blake doesn't say anything to defend himself, but Sebastian rushes forward and punches Blake in the face as I watch in horror. They wrestle onto the ground as Blake blocks most of Sebastian's punches with his arms, but he doesn't fight back or try to stop Sebastian at all.

"She's my fucking sister, not one of your fuck buddies!" Sebastian shouts managing to knock Blake's arm away and landing a sickening punch. I hear Elliot running into the room followed by Luke and Harley. I don't take my eyes away from Sebastian and Blake, as Blake defends himself, while Sebastian tries to get more hits in.

"Stop them!" I shout at my other brothers with tears running down my cheeks. My shouting at them makes Harley finally snap out of shock before he pushes between them and holds Sebastian back.

"What's going on? Calm the fuck down, Seb," Harley says calmly, but I can see the threat in the way he stands holding both of Sebastian's arms at his sides.

"I love her. I'm in love with your sister, and I'm not sorry," Blake says, and his eyes meet mine.

29

IZZY

"Elizabeth, come downstairs!" the angry voice of my foster dad shouts through the house. I groan and look over at my clock to see it's five in the morning. I have four hours until school, and I'll have to clean the whole damn house before I can leave. I roll out of bed to have a quick shower and throw on jeans, a vest, and hoodie before running down the stairs. I stop at the mirror in the hallway, pulling my long, almost-white hair into a ponytail and hoping it doesn't look too messy. The two-bedroom house is a tip, despite the fact I cleaned it yesterday morning, like I do most mornings. Fred, my *lovely* foster dad, is passed out on a stool in the kitchen with his hand wrapped around a vodka bottle. I know better than to talk to him, it's not worth waking him up. So, I start cleaning around him. They kept me up most of the night with their loud music and another party that didn't stop till three in the morning. *Let's not mention the idiots who tried to open my locked door.* I guess I should be thankful that they, at least, feed me for doing the cleaning. I know that if I didn't get up and clean, there would be no food for a week. Finally, at eight, it's all done. I grab my bag, slamming the door on my way out.

As much as I try to forget my living situation, I can't, because every day is a reminder. I've lived with Fred and Vivian since I was fifteen. It's been a nightmare from day one. Sure, they act all lovely and great when social services are around, but, in reality, they use me to clean the house. I just try to stay out of their way. I have six more months till I'm eighteen then I can leave. I'm not sure where, but honestly, anywhere would be better. I have no living family and no money, so I don't have many options other than to find a job quickly and a room to rent. I walk into school thirty minutes later, a little hot from the warm weather we have been having. I glance around at the grammar school which I have to attend. It's this or college, supposedly the grammar school is good for my grades. *But, I have always felt it's more like the better of two evils.*

The day progresses as I would usually expect it to, filled with art and history classes all day. I took a double-A level in art and one in history, which is surprisingly not that boring. Later that day, as I sit at lunch alone like every day, I think of my best friend Tilly. She moved to France two months ago and was the only reason I could deal with this crazy-ass school. It's full of posh idiots whose parents paid to get them in, not like me and Tilly, who actually got straight A's. Tilly really didn't need to study hard like I did, but she did, anyway, and that's why I like her.

I'm pulled from my thoughts by the intercom, "Would Elizabeth Turner come to the main office?"

When it clicks off, I look up to see everyone staring at me. I shrug as I try not to blush. *I hate being the centre of attention.* I walk to the office on the other side of the building after getting my things. I keep thinking of what the hell I've done or if Fred has called to say there is another family emergency at home. Which is usually code for '*I have friends coming to get drunk, and I need the house clean again and didn't notice you had already cleaned*'. I roll my eyes and soon I'm at the office, where I'm told to go straight in by the snooty receptionist.

I walk in the room to see my head teacher behind the desk and the back of a tall man with dark-brown hair tied in a loose knot at the back of his head.

"Come and sit, Elizabeth, there has been some news, and this man has come to talk to you," says my head teacher, but I ignore him and watch as the dark-haired man turns to me.

"It's nice to meet you. You wouldn't believe how long I have looked for you, and it's a little bit of shock to finally meet my sister," the stranger says to me in a deep voice. *Wait sister?*

I turn and look at my head teacher, hoping he will help, but he ignores me and looks out the window. *I guess this is as awkward for him as it is for me.* I look back at the man, taking in his head of dark-brown hair and massive, muscular build to his expensive looking pressed suit. I finally look in his eyes and see the same bright-green eyes I have, looking back at me. I gasp and start to back away into a seat on the couch. I look down at the floor as I try to collect my thoughts. My mother never told me anything about my father, just that I wouldn't want to meet him and left it at that. She passed away a few years ago, four days after my fifteenth birthday. I guessed she would have told me about him when I was older, but who knows? *She never got the chance.*

"Look, I know this is strange, but I am your half-brother, and I have custody of you until you turn eighteen. I've come to take you back home with me," he says like it's an everyday fact. I'm getting the impression not a lot bothers him, and I've only just met him.

I half listen as I'm still trying to take all of this in. A brother, if that isn't enough to deal with. I've then got him adding on the fact that I'm moving. *I should panic and run.* Who knows what he wants or if he is even my brother, but, then again, it can't be worse than where I live now.

"Elizabeth, look at me," my brother says as he picks up on my internal war.

I look up into those familiar, green eyes that show me some kindness. I try to think of more reasons to run, but it seems pointless. *Well, I think I'm going to have to trust him.*

"It's Izzy, my friends call me Izzy. What's your name?" I ask him.

I'm still looking at his face, trying to see the truth behind his words. I get the feeling he is a closed book as far as emotions go, but I can see some kindness, and that's enough for me to try and relax.

"I'm Harley King, nice to meet you Izzy." He smiles, and it takes me a minute to realise he kind of looks like I do in pictures when I smile.

I stand up quickly, putting some distance between us. "What did you mean when you said you would take me back with you and custody?" I try to ask calmly and kind of fail when my voice is high-pitched.

"That you're coming to live with me as you have no other blood relatives as far as I know, so I got custody of you. I have custody of my three younger brothers too. Well, your brothers too," he scratches his head with a huff. I watch as he sits down on the sofa and straightens his suit jacket before saying, "I know this is hard for you to believe, and *trust me,* this whole situation is difficult. Our father is dead. I took over when he died. I was twenty, and the twins, Sebastian and Elliot, were fifteen. Luke was fourteen. It was difficult, but I made it work. I later found out–from a letter from dad's will–about you. It had the results of a DNA test done when you were a baby, and an old address and number of yours. Of course, it's taken me two years to find you due to all the moves you, and your mother, had taken. I'm sorry for your loss by the way."

I nod and sit next to him, taking it all in. *I have four brothers.* I guess he is right about us moving when I think about it. My mother just liked to see new places, and I was taken along for the ride. Yesterday, I had no one, now I have a family, and I am moving away from my crazy, foster family. *This shit seems unbelievable.*

"Alright, I'm going to be honest with you. I've done everything I can to leave my crazy, foster parents. So, this could work for me. I mean moving to your place, and then we can see how things go. I guess I would like to meet the rest of you and learn about you. How old are my brothers now?" I ask looking at Harley, who looks around twenty-three. *So, they can't be that old.*

"The twins are seventeen like you and Luke is sixteen. I'm so glad you'll come. I thought I'd have a massive fight on my hands with getting you to come with me," he says with a grin, which makes me smile too. He stands up, claps his hands together, getting the attention of my head teacher, and starts talking to him about sending my paper work over and the school switch. I notice he makes a very a large payment to the school to help hurry up my paper work. I look at him now in his perfect suit and frown. I glance down at my baggy hoodie and shabby jeans then finally to my worn trainers that I have had for at least two years. *I'm not going to fit into their world.*

As we head to my house in his massive, black SUV–that's shinier than most of the cars in my small town–I sit wondering what Harley will think of my foster parents or their home.

30

IZZY

"Izzy, we need to go soon, but I understand if you want to wait until tomorrow to pack and say your goodbyes," Harley says while pulling the car into the parking space next to the house. I sit back and glance around at the house. The lawn hasn't been done since the last social services inspection six months ago, and it's clear nothing has been done. It has long grass that's mostly weeds, covering the small, front lawn and cracked pavement leading to the door. The house, itself, hasn't been worked on for years, and it's clear from the outside. My lazy and possibly crazy, foster parents wouldn't bother leaving the house to do any work on it. Well, they didn't care enough to make me mow it or risk neighbours seeing me working my ass off for them. It's a nice neighbourhood with decent people living here, and they need to keep up some kind of appearance.

"No. I only have a bag or so of things. So, it will only take me half an hour to pack. Do you want to wait?" I ask, hoping he will stay. I secretly don't want to be alone with them when they find out I'm leaving. They have never hurt me, but throwing things near me and screaming at me is normal for them. I frown, thinking of times when it's worse if they have been drinking, which I'm guessing they have by now. *It is midday.*

"Yes. I need to tell them about you leaving with me," he tells me and then frowns. "Well, your foster parents should have received a phone call or letter explaining anyway," he hesitates before continuing as he stares at the house. "Why have you only got one bag? What about your clothes and, well, girl stuff?" he asks while pulling out the car keys.

I nearly sigh in relief that he's not leaving me here, and I say quietly, "I don't have many clothes or other things,"

I try to get out of the car, not wanting to discuss this anymore, but a large hand on my upper arm gently stops me. He huffs, gaining my attention back to him as he moves his hand.

"Seb is going to love spoiling you with my credit card," he laughs loudly and gets out of the car, too.

I frown at his statement, but my nerves get the best of me and don't let me think about it anymore as I stare up at the home I've lived in for the last few years. So many memories are bad here, but also, in some ways, this place made me stronger. I straighten up and walk into the house with Harley following me. We walk into the living room, where my foster dad is passed out face-down on the sofa with a bottle of vodka in his hand. I'm guessing Vivian is at one of her friends,' as she is nowhere to be seen.

"I wouldn't wake him up if I was you. I'll go and pack," I say in a whisper and shrug at Harley as he glares at Fred on the sofa. I notice how he looks around the room in disgust before smiling at me, but I can see the pity in his eyes.

As I walk past him, he says to hurry up. I suppress a smile at that and run up to my room. I throw my three pairs of jeans, four tops, and my leggings in a bag. I get all my underwear and my necklace from my mother. It's the only thing that my foster parents haven't sold of mine. The memory of my mother comes rushing at me as I hold the necklace.

I know I shouldn't be looking in mum's jewellery box, but everything is so pretty. I'm only seven, so mum won't be too mad. I open the worn, wooden box, and inside are pretty, little earrings I've seen my mom wear, and, in the middle, is a very pretty, purple necklace I've never seen. I pull it out holding it up in the air as it sparkles in the light from the window, making me giggle.

"Elizabeth," the angry voice of my mother makes me jump and turn to see her standing in the doorway to the bedroom. Her white-blonde hair is up in a messy bun from cleaning, and she is wearing a pretty, red dress. Her face softens slightly after a second before she lets out a long breath and comes over to me. She kneels in front of the stool I'm sitting on and takes the necklace out of my hand gently.

"It's real pretty, mummy," I say, frowning at my mummy's sad face.

"It is, isn't it? I haven't looked at this in years. It's called a sapphire," she tells me.

"Who gave you it, mummy?" I ask as she stares at the necklace in her hand. The sapphire is about the size of her thumb and shines like my mummy's blue eyes.

"The man who still holds my heart, baby. I just can't let this go," She whispers the end part to herself, then she stands up, putting the necklace back in her box and holds her hand out to me.

"Do you want to go and get ice cream? Mummy could use some chocolate ice cream," she smiles, making me laugh.

"Yes, mummy," I squeal jumping up and down.

The memory of her fades, leaving only the sadness that she is gone. I kept it hidden well enough because of that memory. I guess I had always hoped it was my dad who gave it to her, but who knows? It looks expensive, but my mum never dated anyone that I saw growing up, so it could be. *I could ask Harley*. I put it in my bag and then go into the bathroom to collect my shampoos, soap, razors, and hairbrush. I chuck those into the bag and look at myself in the full-length mirror. My long, almost white-blond hair is nearly at my waist. Even in a plait like it is now. I have those bright-green eyes, like my brother, and a layer of freckles I'm not a fan of. I'm quite pale, as I don't get out much, but I have a good body. *As my best friend would tell me anyway*. I'm looking at my eyes wondering about my father, when I hear a thump and a man cry out. I race down the stairs finding Harley holding Fred by his neck up against a wall, and Harley's face is close to Fred's.

"Don't speak about my sister like that ever again, or I'll end you. Do you understand me?" he asks.

Fred mumbles a shaken, "Yes."

Harley lets him drop to the floor. He looks back to me with a smile and starts brushing down his suit before asking, "You ready?" I nod, and he turns back to Fred with a scary amount of hate on his face.

"We're going now and don't contact my sister or I'll find you."

With that, he gestures for me to walk out, and I do with my head held high. I say goodbye to my old life and head out into the new.

31

IZZY

We drive for around seven hours towards the Lake District, away from my old life. Harley tells me that we'll be living in a small village called Kendean, where they are all from. Harley continues, telling me that I will be joining the twins in their last year at the local grammar school. The school does the same courses that I am doing now, and I can continue them for the few remaining months I have left. We talk about what I study, I tell him about my love of art and history. I also tell Harley that I want to work with my art when I'm older. I'm surprised when he thinks this is a great idea and can't wait to see my work.

"So, what work do you do?" I ask.

"I own the local gym in the village. It's the only one for miles, so we do good business. Plus, it helps that we all had a very good inheritance." He glances at me before looking back at the road.

"That's why you're all buff then," I joke, and he grins at me.

"Yes, and so are your brothers. You can come any time to build some muscles if you want," he smiles.

"No, I don't do exercise." I laugh at his shocked face. "I'm serious. I can run if I want to, but I get all red and sweaty. Well, I'm lazy."

"You're joking, right? Don't you eat? Because you're quite thin and small," his tone is now serious.

I can understand why, seeing where I came from, but I'm just lucky that I have a good body despite not doing much exercise. *My friend Tilly always used to moan about that.* "I just have good genes I guess. I have a bad addiction to Ben and Jerry's ice cream."

I laugh with Harley when he answers, "It's good that Luke likes that stuff, and it's always in the freezer, then."

"I may like Luke already," I say.

"Do you drive? We live in the middle of nowhere, and without a car, it will be difficult to get around," he says, and I sigh thinking back to Tilly's father who bought me a crash course for my seventeenth birthday from all of them. It was the sweetest thing, even if I could never afford a car and insurance. I passed straight away out of pure luck, I believe, and a few late nights practising in my foster parents' car.

"Yeah, I have a licence," I answer.

"That's great, all the boys have cars, so one of us will be able to drive you anywhere until Seb or I can buy you a new car," he tells me.

"That's too much money," I frown.

Harley laughs at that and we carry on the drive in a comfortable silence. As we pull into the village, we cross over a beautiful, old bridge with a large river running through the town. As we drive further, I notice the small mountains in the background. The town is beautiful even at night-time. It's now close to midnight, I see as I glance at the clock, and I'm hoping to go straight to bed when we get there. *I'm glad we stopped off for some food on the road.*

We pass more country roads and eventually pull into a small road with heavy, black gates which are open. I can see a long road behind them with massive trees on both sides, and it's lit up with large, street lamps.

Harley mutters something about the gates being open when they weren't meant to be and drives up the path. Slowly, the biggest house I've ever seen comes into view. It's beautiful, grey stone even in dim lighting, but when I see all the cars parked in front and hear the loud music blasting from inside it distracts me from the house. *I wonder if this is normal.* I briefly think I have no chance of sleeping until morning as I look at the garage built on the side of the house and then the people flittering around outside. I can't see much in the dark, but it seems to have big windows lining the front of the house.

"For fuck's sake, I leave them for three days and come back to a massive party," Harley says as he jumps out of the car and slams the door.

I go to follow, and he gestures for me to stay behind him. I really don't want to be my brothers right now. *Harley looks scary as hell.* He slams the massive, wooden doors open and pushes drunken people out of the way as I follow him. I can't see or hear much over the amount of people and noise from some loudspeakers that make my ears feel like they are bleeding. I have never been to many parties because I just didn't have the clothes or the time to go to them.

We pass through a dark kitchen which has three

couples making out on the counters. I keep my head down and try not to look around. I do spot the booze everywhere when we pass through a dining room, where there were teenagers dancing on the impressive, wooden table. We eventually make our way into a living area with two massive speakers, one on either side of the largest TV I've ever seen. On screen, is a music channel with almost naked girls dancing. There are three black-leather sofas spread around the TV, and on each is a couple. The room is dark, so I can't see much.

Harley leans into me to shout, "I'm going to turn the electric off in the basement. Stay here, if anyone bothers you tell them you're with me, alright? I'm so sorry about this, Izzy," he says with a frown, taking off his jacket and throwing it on a sofa next to a couple who don't notice.

I nod, "No problem, go." I lean against a wall next to the window in the lounge looking out into the massive garden with a huge tree in the middle. There are lights all up the tree, highlighting a big tree house. The tree house currently has drunken people in it, and I watch as two bottles fall off and smash when they hit the ground.

Harley's going to kill our brothers.

Printed in Great Britain
by Amazon